Naked City

Short Stories

route 15

First published by Route
PO Box 167, Pontefract, WF8 4WW
e-mail: info@route-online.com
web: www.route-online.com

ISBN: 1 901927 23 7

Editors:
Anthony Cropper and Ian Daley

Photography by
Kevin Reynolds
www.kevinreynolds.co.uk

Photographer's Assistant:
Katy Reynolds

Cover Design
Andy Campbell
www.absolutely-nothing.com

With thanks to:
Bob Ashby, Ian Bowers, Julia Cropper, Isabel Galán, Claire Goater,
Steve Goodfellow, Roger Green, Rachel Healfield, Chris Howson,
Tracey L Jones, Nick Lewis, Evie Morissette, Simon Naylor and
Mathew Seaward. We'd also like to thank The Arts Cafe Bar, The Corn
Exchange, Nautilus and The Leeds Guide, with a special thanks to Dan
Jeffrey.

Printed by Bookmarque, Croydon

A catalogue for this book is available from the British Library

Route is an imprint of ID Publishing
www.id-publishing.com

This book was possible thanks to support from
Arts Council England

Inside Naked City

*Presented here are two collections of
short stories and a selection of photographs*

Naked City

This powerful collection of short stories takes us inside the
modern city. Perhaps nothing illustrates the current climate
of social change more than the renaissance of our cities,
with the introduction of new architecture, city apartments,
bar culture and new lifestyle possibilities. These stories
capture the spirit of the times with a telling look at how
change affects the way we live our lives.

Naked City Photographs

When approaching this brief, photographer Kevin
Reynolds was faced with the dilemma of the inevitable
comparison to Spencer Tunick's images of thousands of
nude volunteers, and also the *Calendar Girls* phenomenon.
To create a more original body of work, Reynolds shot
images of the naked subjects in everyday situations
throughout the city. All models are volunteers, shot on the
run, without the protection of elaborate set-ups.

This Could Be Anywhere

Seven short stories from an impressive selection of new
writers. This collection offers a progression of stories
drawn from young family life, inter-cut with comical
snapshots of the single lifestyle.

Contents

Part I - Naked City

Part II - This Could Be Anywhere

Part I

Naked City

Crumpet
Malcolm Aslett

Mark and Ingrid might have married but for their views on how to butter a crumpet. There were other minor issues of dissatisfaction in the manner of human tastes and frailty: Ingrid smoked, and Mark thought 'housework' was taking your bike to bits in the kitchen. But really, if we are to believe what they tell people, it was the crumpets that were the killer in a relationship that had started passionately and with promise.

There was nothing unfamiliar about the situation. They had met on holiday in Greece and when they had returned home Mark (engineering student/biker/every mother's son) rode six hundred miles every Friday to stay each weekend with Ingrid (biologist/Londoner/two years older) because he thought she was the best thing since sliced bread (white/bleached flour/family size). Now Ingrid was to see him on his home turf. She caught the train to Newcastle, visiting the north for the first time in her life, with the same kind of expectations adventurous Victorians had entertained when travelling to Stamboul on the Orient Express. Mark met her at Central Station. They kissed demonstratively. He took her bag, which was surprisingly large and heavy, and she scanned the locals to spot any ragged waifs gnawing at morsels in doorways or pot-bellied men with coal dust on their faces. It was all eerily normal.

'It's clean, isn't it?' she asked, surprised.

Mark thought she was making remarks about the architecture.

'Yes. They sandblasted it a few years ago. All the stonework. And cleaned up the girders and trusses and repainted them.'

Then he worried he might be sounding dull and hurriedly thought up a lame joke.

'We know how to show a girder a good time up here!'

Ingrid was so pleased to see him she laughed as if it was funny. They linked arms round each other's waist though this was plainly awkward. Mark leaned into her face to balance up the weight of the bag and Ingrid, standing half an inch taller, had to remodulate all relevant body parts to fit up against his side and walk at the same time. She ignored the discomfort in favour of a display of affection and waited till they had cleared the building before she found some excuse to stop and check that her lighter was still in her pocket and then hold his hand instead.

Mark lived near the quayside in a converted warehouse with wooden doors at inhuman heights and the remnants of pulleys and stumpy projections on the peeling face of the building. There were cobbles underfoot and to either side were the shells of guttered buildings with rough grasses and hardy looking flowers emerging through the cracks in the concrete like the survivors of mini-earthquakes. The River Tyne showed through the gaps at unpredictable moments and seagulls perched on rooftops with the confidence of predators. It made Ingrid believe she was somewhere she was not supposed to be, somewhere out of bounds. But the city centre was a ten-minute walk and the Tyne Bridge was close enough to cast a shadow on the bedroom window round about teatime. And it was the bedroom where they spent the afternoon.

The blue sky was flat and still against the panes. A cloud pushed past on its way south, sluggish as a tourist out window-shopping. They lay underneath a single sheet and the temperature of the air seemed to drop five degrees in as many seconds as the shadow of the bridge crept across the wall. Mark had his left arm under her head, crooked to take in her right breast, his hand tingling with numbness. He didn't care to move an inch. Mark was clingy. He wanted to be holding her at every moment. It didn't bother Ingrid. She actually liked it, most of the time. There was no doubt in her mind that he was besotted with her. He was that northern all-or-nothing type of man who believed people said what they meant if they looked you in the eye and if you fell in love with a girl it was because she was the one for you. An innocence based on a train of social accidents and whatever was showing on television at the time of his childhood. In Mark's case this had been a disproportionate number of Hollywood films of the forties. He had a moral framework that, if dismantled, could have been packed into boxes with stencilled lettering reading: *'Labour Party'*, *'Meat and Two Veg'*, *'That Book I Read (I forget the title)'*. But as well as these there would be a smaller, more carefully packed item bearing the words: *'Katherine Hepburn/Ingrid Bergman – the Sacred and the Profane'*, for they were as good and as bad as he could imagine women to be. For her part Ingrid enjoyed this unsophisticated understanding of, not only the world, but also herself. It was a comfort to be thought of in such uncomplicated terms (Good, Honest, Clever, Beautiful). Besides, she felt comfortable with the power that was contingent to being a young man's lover, knowing that if his thoughts could somehow be made transparent and light passed through them, they would cast sepia images displaying a panoptikon dedicated to her face and form upon every wall. Well yes, sex and sport would be on display too. He was a regular geordie lad, after all. And as she had been through it all before - several times - she could enjoy it all with the confidence that only time-honoured experience or complete ignorance can provide. She made a shivering sound, an intake of breath.

'Y' cold?' he asked.

'Mmmm!'

Mark unclasped his arms and leaned over his side of the bed to fish up the eiderdown from the floor. Ingrid felt the weighty coolness as it came across her and flicked her feet, tail-like, to have it settle farther down. She shivered again.

'I'm hungry.' Her voice was just the right side of babyish.

'You want something to eat?'

'Mmmm!'

'That can be arranged.'

'W't'ya got?'

Mark twisted his face and pretended he had little in the house. He was *so* easy to read this was actually a waste of time but Ingrid politely played along. He had been excited about the visit for two weeks and stocked up with all sorts of goodies he thought would be treats, things he had never tried before but hoped that his first experience of them would become part of their history as a couple. The difficulty was, the flat didn't have a cooker. His kitchen consisted of a kettle, a toaster, cups and plates that had been given away once too often and several bent pieces of metal he referred to nostalgically as 'the family silver'.

He gave her shoulder a long goodbye kiss and slid out of bed.

'I can't find me trousers,' he told her, rooting through the bits of clothing strewn on the floor.

'Well where's the last place you had them?' she teased.

'On me legs.'

Ingrid cuddled into the duvet and chuckled while Mark picked up the long sleeved t-shirt he had been wearing and stuck his legs through the arms and pulled it up tight muttering: 'Designer swimwear!'

He waddled into the bare-brick loft that served as living room, dining room, study, kitchen and garage space for his bike and kayak

– the bedroom was simply two thin plywood walls that boxed in a corner of the space that had once been the ground floor of a warehouse.

She lit a cigarette while he was gone. The bed had no headboard and she stacked both pillows against the wall so she could sit up. She entertained herself by noting all the objects being used for something other than their original intention: a doorframe acting as a wardrobe held up by stanchions with a thick dowel bearing the hangers, a beer can holding pens and pencils, a wooden fruit crate on its side with a mix of shoes in it and books on top. If a little more care had been taken it all would have looked artlessly arty, but the purpose was so unremittingly functional and so apparent was it that the bare minimum of effort had been used to achieve the end result that it made the room appear slightly sad and uncared for. She played a different game:

Q. If this room was a pair of shoes what type would it be? She toyed with the idea of Wellingtons with laces but finally decided it wouldn't be any kind of footwear but rather the box they came in. When she heard him preparing to come back she remembered he would make faces at the smoke so she jumped out of bed and yanked at the bottom of the sash window. It would not budge. But the shaking brought the top sash crashing down and cracked a pane. She was back under the covers and looking supremely innocent when he came through the door holding a tray heavy with cups and bowls and objects wrapped in bags and greasy paper. He nodded his head in the direction of the window.

'I thought I heard a crash. It's forever doing that. Hope you didn't get a fright.'

She shook her head, her eyes wide, and changed the subject.

'What *have* we got here?'

She made space upon the bed for him to place it in the centre then started ripping at the paper and bags without further ceremony.

'Oh, *garlic olives*! Mmmm, and *brie*? And... *brown* cheese? My almost favourite.'

'The girl said it was Norwegian.'

'Ah, the *fjords*!' she said in her best travel programme English.

'Ah, the Austin Allegros!' he countered.

Ingrid laughed aloud. Sometimes she didn't understand his humour but she laughed with the enthusiasm of the good sport.

'Oh, and what's this?'

'It said clams on the tin but they look just like cockles t' me.'

'You were ripped off, eh?'

She took a sip of the Bulgarian wine and made a discreet face.

'And crumpets. Mmm. Have you anything to put on them?'

'I've put it on. Butter.'

'It must have melted.'

'Of course! You have to put it on when it's straight out of the grill so that it melts.'

She cut a large wedge of Brie and pressed at it with the knife to get it to stick to the crumpet. Then she took a large mouthful and immediately decided to ask a question.

'Sho whatsh nesht?'

'Didn't they teach you to not talk with your mouth full in your house?'

'Itsh not full. Look!'

She took another large bite and then squeezed in yet more, her cheeks bulging.

'Gnow itsh full,' she told him with satisfaction.

They were both laughing, Ingrid near to choking on crumbs. They flopped back on the bed, Ingrid turned on her stomach with her head over the edge and her shoulders trembling with suppressed giggles. She put her hand in front of her mouth and let the food fall into it. Still shaking she bent an arm to pull a serviette from the tray and wrapped the offending pieces around it and dropped it onto the floor.

'That's disgusting!' Mark told her admiringly.

The situation inevitably led to more lovemaking. By the time they got out of bed and dressed again the sun was down and the sky outside grained with the particles of a starry night showing through the twilight.

Ingrid was up and ready for a change of pace.

'I'll make some crumpets, shall I?' she asked him.

'That's alright. I'll do it.'

She was out the door of the bedroom before he realised. Her voice echoed from the large space beyond. 'No, that's OK. You get a shower. You're *sweaty!*'

Mark dutifully picked fresh clothes off a hanger and went to the bathroom to shower and shave. When he got out he found the dining table - an old tongue-and-groove door on a pair of trestles- was set up with coffee and cups and the remains of the previous feast but looking neater and more expensive. As he sat down she came over with a plate of crumpets.

'Here we go.'

He dabbed at one with a finger.

'You've let them get cold.'

She looked hurt and put an arm over his shoulder.

'That's no *biggy*, is it? You can still put things on them. Try it!' she told him with a voice oozing reasonableness.

She sat down next to him and immediately put a thick spread of soft margarine on hers. Then came a brick of brown cheese and a dollop of cherry jam. She took a bite and made noises.

'Mmmm!'

Mark caught himself acting peevishly and tried to correct it.

'Alright, alright. I get the picture.'

He made up a twin to Ingrid's crumpet and started to nibble at the edges.

'Mmmmm?' Ingrid asked.

'Hmmm,' he told her.

'And what does that mean?'

He leaned over and kissed her.

'It means I need a drink.'

Ingrid had spoken to Mark two days earlier on the phone. When she had asked if there was anything to do in the town he had proudly told her that Newcastle city centre was the most policed area in Europe on a Saturday night.

'Um, well. Call me old-fashioned but that doesn't make this girl sit up and whoop.'

'Right, right. I see what you mean. Well then, there's an old cruise liner on the river that they've made into a bar and restaurant.'

'Oh that might be fun,' she told him. 'What's that like?'

'I don't know. I've never been.'

After further probing it was apparent that pretty much all Mark knew of the nightlife was his local pub on the quayside.

So now they found themselves on the quayside coming out of the selfsame pub. The air had turned cold. A cutting breeze brought the smell of the sea as it came barreling up the River Tyne and turned Ingrid's bare arms into goose bumps in the time it took to remember where she was.

'Ooof! That's cold.'

'Here, you can put this on,' Mark told her, dropping his leather jacket over her shoulders.

'Oh, thanks! Oh! That's better!' she told him and squeezed

tightly and thankfully onto his slim hips.

Mark guided them up steep streets to the town centre, past loudly singing gangs of boys and girls in thin bright clothes, dressed as if on a holiday in the Mediterranean on a balmy summer's evening. A stately crescent of buildings led to a broad pedestrian area with a kind of Nelson's Column at its head.

'Who's that on top?' Ingrid asked peering up.

'Earl Grey. Inventor of the tea bag, legend has it.'

'Finally. A monument for someone who really provided something significant to our way of life.'

By the reflective walls of the Eldon shopping centre a fight broke out between two men dressed in identical football strips and who were, quite possibly, twins. The sound of the smack of fist against flesh travelled with unique clarity in the broad streets rumbling with human voices. Mark was curious and slowed to watch but Ingrid pulled him in the other direction. At another corner they stopped to get their bearings.

'Where does this street lead?'

'This way takes you to the bridge. Do you want to see it?'

He had asked her this three or four times since she had arrived and it was gradually dawning on her that he had some affection for the grimy old thing.

'Yeah, sure!' she told him, her tone a mixture of enthusiasm and disinterest.

In the pocket of the jacket Ingrid was wearing there was a piece of tissue with something inside it that kept pricking her finger. She had been toying with it all the while and now pulled it out.

'What's this?'

Mark took a moment to remember.

'I nearly forgot. I picked it up for you at the station while I was waiting.'

She unwrapped the tissue, which she stuck in her cuff, and held in her hand a badge in the shape of the Tyne Bridge.

'That's sweet.'

'Just a memento,' he told her softly. 'It's a three-month anniversary present.'

'I like it. Are you going to pin it on me?'

They stopped so that she could unzip the jacket a few inches and he awkwardly pinned it to her top. They kissed for a little while and then silently agreed to walk on.

Ingrid was feeling relaxed and happy. She rubbed at the badge through the coat as if she were polishing it and then took the tissue out of her cuff to wipe her nose that was now feeling sniffly.

'It reminds me. My sister was in a coffee shop near where she works when she sneezed and some stranger offered her his cotton handkerchief. So she took it. The next day he was in the coffee shop again and he came over and gave her a crocodile he had made out of paper and then walked away without saying anything. The following day he gave her an old leather button. She was with her friends and he was always on his own so they never really talked. But he kept giving her these little presents.'

'So what was that all about?'

'Well, the fourth day he brought her an apple and the fifth day a tiny little wooden boat. When she got the wooden boat she asked him out and they started seeing each other. But he still kept giving her something different every day – an old penny, a tin soldier.'

'Where did he get all this stuff?'

'I don't know. Second-hand shops. That sort of thing. But the point is, she felt there was something behind it that he wouldn't tell her. He was a journalist as it turned out. A bit of an intellectual. And he liked crime stories – the sort with puzzles and clues in them.'

'So what? This was all part of the plan for the perfect murder?'

'No, not quite, Mister Cynical. When they had been seeing each other for *sixty days* he gave her a diamond ring.'

'An *engagement* ring?'

'Yes! He proposed. Do you not get it?' she asked, and then started counting off the things on her fingers: 'Cotton, paper, leather, fruit…'

Mark looked completely baffled so Ingrid put him out of his misery.

'They're the traditional gifts you give when you're celebrating the years of your marriage. The first year is cotton, the second is paper, and so on.'

'Oh. And did she accept? After two months?'

'Yes. They've been married five years now. She's just had her first baby. A little boy.'

'So what was all this with the gifts? Just a puzzle to get her interested?'

'He told her later that he knew he wanted to marry her the first time he set eyes on her.'

'*Good grief!*'

Ingrid elbowed him in the ribs.

'Don't sound so disgusted. It's quite romantic for this day and age. Don't you think?'

'It's quite…*something.*'

She tried to elbow him again and he manoeuvred out of the way to avoid it. They were approaching the Tyne Bridge and a drizzly wind started buzzing around them. Ingrid shivered audibly and Mark came tight up to her back and wrapped his arms around her.

'D'you like the idea?'

'Of what?' she asked cautiously.

'Of having a family?'

'Mmmm. I love visiting my sister and being with her family. And her little boy, Sebastian. He's such a goofy looking thing. I'd like a boy of my own, I think. I like goofy looking boys!'

'Ha, ha!' he said without laughing.

'In fact I've always had a thing about boys with their front teeth missing. Little boys, I mean. They look so cute.'

'It's probably why people become dentists. A maternal urge.'

She dug him in the ribs again and tried to pull away but he held onto her.

'So what do you think this fleece jacket is made out of? Leather, cotton lining with a stainless steel zip? That might count for years one, nine and eighty-six. If you want to keep it.'

Ingrid turned her head to see what the look was on his face but the glaring street lamp behind him obliterated any detail. Still, the moment seemed comfortable enough. She smiled happily and they kissed. It was like sealing a contract. A pity it all had to change when Mark was suddenly overcome by a peculiar atavism. Modern research might explain it by pinpointing an unusual shaped gene lodged deep in the DNA, a biological mechanism that cranks into action to trigger an ancient piece of human behaviour when the male believes he has made special claim to the female and she has given some provisional show of acceptance. It may or may not require a bridge for the purpose but the prop was used in this instance.

'You know what we used to do when we were kids?' he asked out of the blue.

'Umm, kids stuff?' she guessed brightly.

'Right first time. Only, when we were on the bridge…'

He stopped talking to hoist himself on the wall, placing one foot square in the middle and bringing his knee next to it.

'…we used to try and walk along the wall…!'

'No, Mark. *Please!*'

He put his arms out wide like a tightrope walker and stood up shakily.

'It's not difficult,' he told her. But his voice was now edged with doubt as the wind buffeted at his shirt and swept the hair across his eyes. The trouble was, now that he had started he felt obliged to go at least a few steps. He inched one leg out and moved forward with the grace of a peg-legged pirate walking the plank. The river below was invisibly black and the wall before him criss-crossed with dark shadow and white light creating an optical illusion consisting of indefinable areas of space and solidity. He decided he would make three quick steps and get down. Best not make a *total* fool of himself. As well as that he decided that if he slipped, all he had to do was grab hard and hold fast to the wall. He took another step. An ill-intentioned gust caught him and in a fit of aeronautical whimsy began to twist his body into the elegant curves of a propeller. Mark felt himself borne by the convoluted force and flung his arms forwards to grip the wall. The confusion of light and shadows swinging towards his face was a puzzle he had too little time to solve. His forehead hit the wall with a mighty crack while his body twisted and rolled onto the pavement side of the bridge. Mark's head was swimming with the blow. The one thought in his mind still working was to hold onto the wall and save himself from falling into the river. As his body rolled his fingers found the edge of the kerb and he hugged his body tightly against the paving stones, gripping the kerb with all his might, for in his mind he was dangling a hundred feet up against the side of the bridge on a merciless night.

Ingrid rushed up to him.

'Oh, Mark! Are you alright?'

It was a mystery of nature why her voice should be behind him.

'I…must…pull…!'

He tried dragging his body up to safety but couldn't find the strength. His eyes were closed as tight as knots and his arms seemed utterly wasted.

Ingrid tried to help him up and tugged at his waist.

He gave a yelp as he felt her pulling him off the bridge. When she tried unclasping his fingers from the kerb he began to panic.

'No! No…! Stop. What you *doing*? I'll fall!'

At that point a taxi cruising past slowed to a crawl and pulled up. The driver got out and ran over.

'Need a hand, love?'

'No, that's alright,' Ingrid told him, sounding flustered.

He ignored this and bent down to get a whiff of Mark's breath. Satisfied that he wasn't simply inebriated he gave him a fatherly pat on the back.

'Here, love. Get his other arm.'

The two of them managed to heave him to his feet. He stood up, utterly dazed, his eyes focused on a point somewhere between his nose and four days ago.

The taxi driver seemed genuinely concerned.

'Looks like he's got concussion. What happened?'

Ingrid shook her shoulders.

'He slipped and banged his head.'

The driver gave a sigh as if this were so terribly sad.

'Let's get him to the infirmary,' he told Ingrid. And the two of them led him to the cab in baby steps.

'Where's me *bike*?' Mark asked them. 'Don't forget me *bike*.'

Ingrid sat in the waiting room for four hours. It was normally her habit to carry a book wherever she went and it made her sulky to be reduced to reading two-page magazine articles that promised to change her life forever. Sitting opposite her was a bleary-eyed young man in a white shirt with a swathe of crimson down the front, swaying in his chair like washing on a line, while next to him was a heavy set girl in an impressively short leather dress who sporadically burst into tears.

An ambulance took them home. Mark still seemed stunned but was talking normally again though they were really too tired to say anything. Ingrid helped him undress and got him into bed. She had a long bath to warm herself up and by the time she climbed in next to him he was asleep. The room was uncomfortably cold with blasts of rain-flecked air from the open window. She got up and struggled for several minutes to close it, before surrendering and putting on one of Mark's thick woolly jumpers that smelled of machine oil. Then Mark began snoring. She had never known him to do that. Unable to sleep she got her cigarettes and lighter from under the bed and lit up. Her nose was blocked and her throat feeling sore and the smoke was no comfort.

'I know where this is going,' she said to herself.

When he saw her off the next day it was an uncomfortable affair.

'Right. Are you busy next weekend?' he had asked her.

'Umm, yes. Sorry. I promised my sister I'd go round,' with enough evasion in the way she had said it to make him drop the subject.

There was a hug and a kiss of sorts where she blew her nose before and after. The train pulled out and that was the last they saw of each other. The break-up came via a string of telephone calls that were like a drawing of a series of telegraph poles in perspective, gradually diminishing into nothing. Within the year Ingrid had rekindled a relationship with Carla, an Italian language teacher she had lived with at college. This lasted till an argument over the splitting of the bill in a Barcelona tapas bar two years later. The death of her sister the following autumn was the most tragic thing that had ever happened to her, but she had always had a crush on her brother-in-law and married him after a semi-respectable eleven months. Mark bought a bigger bike and kept it until he married a local girl and procreation demanded he swap it for a Volvo estate.

Mark forgot altogether the incident on the bridge. As far as he was concerned she had been his first real love but when it came to the matter of explaining old photographs dug out of shoeboxes it was: 'Ingrid. She was smashing. Really good fun. But I'll tell you what really bugged me about her was the way she made crumpets. She'd let them get cold and put *wadges* of margarine on them so it was, like, half an inch thick with the stuff, and then eat them in one mouthful!' And then he would shiver, as if someone were stepping on his grave.

And Ingrid. You could never really know what Ingrid was thinking. But she had a display case on the wall of the dining room. It was perhaps a printer's old box for holding type and now each small space held a single item that she had collected to represent each year of her life. In the twenty-fifth compartment was a badge of the Newcastle Bridge. If, as it sometimes happened, a flirtatious dinner guest asked her to list the provenance of the trinkets on display she would explain the year as follows:

'My geordie boyfriend. He was terribly sweet and rode a motorbike and ate his crumpets in a funny way.'

'*Funny?*' the guest would ask leering.

'Mmmm. It was all he ever ate, really. I think I would have married him if he had made a better crumpet.'

All eyes would turn to her husband while the men barracked him.

'Myself,' he would tell them earnestly, 'I'm an English muffin man!' and usually everyone would laugh and they could change the subject to the next item in her history box and on through the years past a silver safety pin and her little boy's front tooth.

Muff-Diving Over the Fish Market

Char March

I can't believe I'm allowing myself to orgasm while the clipped fifties accent of the World Service burbles. They are describing the Queen's outfit as she opened some community hospital in Ghana this week. I don't think I'll ever be able to lick a stamp in quite the same way again.

We make a great porn movie for the old guy I see across the courtyard – oblivious under his battered lampshade with the slightly swaying low-watt bulb. He's coughing, scratching a bit, making a strong brew of Typhoo, wishing his bladder would let him sleep right through for once. A stooped silhouette against his peeling seventies bedsit.

She's certainly a worker this one. A definite Teutonic efficiency - and prepared to put in long working hours down below. And we have been at it for hours. From Sailing By and The Shipping Forecast right through the World Service to finally collapse just as Prayer for the Day clicks into Farming Today. For she is fixated on British radio, Hoovers up the BBC output 24/7, insists it just isn't the same listening via broadband back in Berlin.

Just across Kirkgate, the shutters start clashing up. The fish-trolleys buck over kerbs slewing crushed ice. The fleshily pink men curse-heave the awkward plastic crates. The whizz I had early yesterday evening finally finally finally lets me shut my eyes.

***

And now her eyrie bedroom is drenched with sun. It's six floors up - an old repository space perched on top of a stack of dank solicitors' offices and evil-smelling dentists' with, at street level, a piercing parlour, a Goth clothes shop and a Chinese chippy. Sandwiched between the zeppelin splendour of the Corn Exchange and the ornately spired skyline of the market, this forgotten block quietly crumbles. Trust Ms Audi to spot its potential.

The sun floods through the massive new Veluxes, makes the huge expanse of wooden floor glow - look lit from inside. The whole flat is suffused with the scent of pine resin. The creamy-yellow dust from her recent frenzy of sanding is everywhere – a fine downy layer over the few strategically-placed pieces of furniture, over each gleamingly expensive appliance. I can taste its woody bite right back into my throat. It is smeared into our hair, dried into our sweat, has been ground into sandy ripples over her sheets. It gives this high place a strangely beach feel. And the briny scents rising from the fish market add that certain seaside something. The calls of the Big Issue sellers on Vicar Lane double as seagulls.

She slips her silk dress on to pad through to the kitchen to get the espresso machine wheezing, then disappears into the shower room. Drifting through the tang of pine and dark coffee, I smell the cinnamon of Ayurvedic toothpaste – is this her one nod towards healthy living? I've no idea. I hear the shower blast out, and immediately roll off the bed to the stack system and at last gag Radio Four. I pillage her cds – Goldfrapp, Asian Dub Foundation, Monolake, Zwei Raum Wohnung – how can she possibly prefer the whining dirge of You and Yours to this stuff?!

I lie back as Monolake takes off, drowning out the shower that is busy robbing her of her cloak of honeyed sweat and sawdust.

We breakfast on espresso and rank cigarettes she says she got last week on a business trip to St Petersburg. *Wow, don't you get around* – I say, pretending to be entirely unimpressed. There is a pause. *I prefer it here* – she says. *Yeah* – I say, not even attempting to sound as if I believe her. She looks at me with her cool grey eyes. The colour of Wehrmacht uniform. *Well* – I say – *you wouldn't be saying that if you'd had to grow up in Seacroft, or Harehills, or Beeston, or Armley.*

I don't know these places – she says – *it is here I like.* And she just carries on looking.

I've always been a sucker for endless afternoons of crappy world war two movies. Raus, raus, schnell, Britischer Scheinhund. The stupid German guards always looking the wrong way, the smirking blonde Gestapo agent relishing the torture of the plucky Brit, the one decent German officer who is ashamed of the excesses, the list-making German bureaucrats who tot up the price to be got from the boiled down soap......and from my grandfather's gold tooth, and from my great aunt's cardboard suitcase, and from the hair shaved off my five cousins' heads.

I look around her new space. The sparkling appliances, the quality of everything, the clean economy of line, the tastefulness, the class, the sheer ease of it. She reaches over towards me. I jump up, lock myself in the shower room, stare into the mirror to try to find something. Can't.

She calls through the door to me that she is going out to buy some fish, fruit, have a wander through the stalls. She waits for an answer. I wait for her to leave. She told me last night that the sheer tackiness of the market utterly delights her. It seems they don't have our sort of tat in Berlin.

I stand, her shower pounding steam over me. I am at the parade ground in the Nordhausen KZ where sixteen members of my family were marched, where each were screamed into lines, into lorries, into cattle trucks, each recorded as they set out on their various journeys – to Theresenstadt, to Treblinka, to Bergen Belsen. And there I am, sixty years later, hands trembling around a menthol king-sized, being told by a shame-faced young German attendant – the same one who had helped me find my family name, sixteen times, in the archive lists – that *it is forbidden to smoke in the museum vicinity for it is all buildings of wood and there is fire danger.*

***

I have opened every drawer and gone through every cupboard. I search methodically, diligently, but I don't know what it is I want to find…. or not find. I stuff some of her cds into my handbag, and a packet of dope I find in the vast Smeg. As I pull on my clothes (it always feels weird dressing in club gear in broad daylight) I gnaw on a massive wedge of emmental, try a forkful of fresh Krautsalat nach Hausfrauenart, spit it out in the sink. Then I grab up my jacket and turn. She is watching me. The cool grey following my flickering anxiety. Carefully, slowly, she walks over. Presses some switches. Goldfrapp dies, Brain of Britain takes over, with Robert Robinson asking in that inanely intense way if we know who Beethoven dedicated his umpteenth concerto in twang minor to. I want to look away from the cool grey - to walk away. She pulls open the Smeg, starts to unload the two bags she carries. Unwraps a pain au chocolat, still warm, from a monogrammed paper bag – Harvey Nicks. Yeah, she's really been slumming it down there. She presses it to my lips. I resist, watching, watching the cool grey of her. Then I open my mouth, bite into the buttery flakes. She tears the rest of the pastry off against my teeth and drops it onto the basalt countertop. She pushes her lips against mine, nuzzling with her tongue.

She'd been sat there for an hour, parked opposite Queen's Court. Just watching.

Lower Briggate – being the gay end of town – is not exactly brightly lit, but even so, I'd seen her sitting there. Well, it was the big Audi that I clocked first of course - not that many posh cars dare to park down this way. But I'd clocked her too. Into her forties, a bit on the rail-thin side, but still taking care of herself. Tall – I could tell even though she was sitting. Blonde – but definitely not out of a bottle. And definitely not my sort. And that's why I clocked her. Cos I'd decided to throw in the towel with going for 'my sort'. So I clocked her – did I say that already? Well, she stood out like the proverbial. Trying so desperately to be invisible. Sat there in shades for godssake. On Lower Briggate. In February. At half eleven at night. Even I don't pose quite that absurdly. And the positioning of the car was a dead give-away. Especially her edging it backwards when the Fiesta behind her pulled away – that way she could get a clear view into the Queen's courtyard where, let's face it, quite a bit of the action goes on…or rather goes down.

So, I decided to give her a bit more of a floorshow. Told some of the tastiest guys and gals who were inside to strut their best positions outside. Grumbles of course – this is February, and Leeds is hardly St Tropez. But I'd got a free bag of whizz from Daniel for his latest web redesign, so I doled it out liberally and they complied. And she got her fill. Or so I'd thought.

But there she was the next night. Greedy - I thought. So I slipped out the side way and came stalking up on her blind side while she's guzzling in the view waiting for some more action, and in I slips – passenger door unlocked. Clearly she's not a local. No-one in their right mind would do that on Lower Briggate.

And she turns round all fear and indignation and her mouth

open. So I snogged her. And I expected a bit of a fight. But she just – well, I thought she just sort of relaxed. But turns out she passed out – straight out. Off like a light switch. Weird. But quite sexy in a bizarre sort of a way.

I couldn't get her to come into the club when she came round a few seconds later. She was too busy rolling round all those delicious Kraut consonants, telling me she seems to have lost her way and is just a businesswoman and she wants to just find a restaurant to eat. *At nearly midnight?* I ask. All wide-eyed innocence. *And besides. What were you doing here last night then?* And do you know, she blushed. I thought no-one did that anymore. I thought it was just kind of Victorian or something. But up she rose, all rosy and bashful. Well sexy. And I says - *I thought you Krauts had a lot more bottle – you've invaded the world twice after all.* She looked shocked. Hurt even. So I laughed – to show her it was a joke…sort of.

***

Afterwards we sat, each in her own aloneness, an enormous half-metre between us on the back seat. Each in her own bubble-world – mine of fears and doubts. Hers? I had no idea. I remember hoping that this was cool, a good laugh. Because, after all, how could it not be? I'd just earned a hundred quid from Sals and Nic after all. This was what it was all about, wasn't it? Having a wild time. A good laugh. A good laugh.

And so we sat there. Her pulling occasionally at the hem of her washed-silk skirt. Us both listening to the disjointed, but deepening frog chorus of the bouncers punctuated with drunken screeches as ladettes fell off their trotters all up and down Boar Lane.

And all I felt was bewildered, which felt all wrong – and bizarre. Me? Bewildered? What was all this about?

It had been a dare. Sals and Nic betting me a donkey I wouldn't go out there and have her on her leather upholstery. Sals had brought up the Kraut bit. *Go on – do your bit towards reconciliation.* And we'd nearly pissed ourselves laughing. It would be a real blast. A good laugh. Sals had spotted her Audi, her tall smooth height, her tiny Catholic cross. Her consonants had simply confirmed her Teutonicness.

It wasn't meant to mean anything – to anyone. And yet here we were forty-eight hours later. Here we were. Es muss zusammen uns bringen.

I'd moved out of Moortown years before, and horrified my parents on my next visit back – swathed in a Palestinian headscarf, clutching my plastic Buddha handbag, and talking about my new all-day-Saturday job. Mum had wept and gone to re-polish the kosher crockery. Dad had yelled at me in Yiddish and sworn at me in German and begged me in English. I'd said I was fed up with the silences and all the stored-up stuff and that they had to move on, and - if they couldn't - I had.

I'd learnt T'ai Chi, read the Koran, was a regular at Leeds Parish Church carol concert, been to classes about the Ba'Hai faith, written a humanist funeral into my will. And here I was standing in a German Catholic dyke's shower having flashbacks to the concentration camps and wanting to hack this tender woman to bits and force out of her that her Dad had been in the SS and and and and cry. Which I did, spluttering out the pain au chocolat, sobbing wildly and running round and round her flat. Wailing - until long after her arms closed round me.

***

It's late again. The Velux above us has turned into dark velvet. A roadsweeper chugs and fizzes its brushes up a silent Vicar Lane, snuffling amongst the empty cans and chip-papers. The World

Service is just a low burble. And she is leaning over me, parting my lips with the tips of her neatly manicured fingers. She feeds me a square of slightly melted Ritter-Sport Schokolade. Joghurt flavour. I've always loathed this stuff - I'm definitely a Yorkie girl - so how come it tastes so good?

And how come, with this woman who I barely know, I've just had one of those once-in-a-blue-universe orgasms – the ones that leave you unable to move, or speak, or even breathe very well. And that don't seem to be anything to do with any of your separate bits - but are a definition of that strange truism: the sum of the parts being greater than…. It infused all of me – in fact filled the whole room, the whole flat, poured out of her sixth floor windows, overflowed down the pocked and rusting fire escape, filled the graffitied courtyard till it was a huge square bowl of glistening silver, then mercuried out over the roofs to waterfall down and down, crashing in massive waves along Vicar Lane, down Kirkgate, belting into the market's entrances, burrowing up through the Arcades to sluice through Briggate, smashing Harvey Nicks glass frontage, tsunamis chasing to catch up with each other till every street in central Leeds is submerged in silken water, just the two gold owls hooting out the submarine presence of the Civic Hall. And the whole thing just reverberates on and on, out and out – like soundwaves.

I'm being pulled - out of myself, out of the flat and into the vast lake that used to be Leeds. The water closes round me - a cushioned surface of silver and bubbles. It is a satin dress, heavy, shining, sliding round my limbs, billowing up round my face, pulling me under. And I realise that I am smiling – a weird half-smile. I can feel it tug my lips as if I am somewhere else. I must look like some weirdo Mona Lisa. The thought wrenches me, threatens to pull me gasping, spluttering from the lake. But I am stone and calm again. Sinking, super-dense now and accelerating down. Super-gravity, and yet floating. Time is distorting, like at the edge of a black hole. I spin in slow-mo, the curving side of a vortex. Cool, calm, all sounds muffled, the water blurring and blurring my stone eyes. And all around the ripples ring out and out and out and out and out......

But she's worried. I'm lying too still. A hand - gentle - on some part of me. The catch in her low voice. *You are...alive still?*

And I have to speak. Such an effort - to form words with my stone mouth, to open it under all this lake, to be heard in this deep stillness.

But I reassure her, and then - wonder of wonders - am able to stay deep, still, calm, feeling the O ringing and ringing – me, the room, the world.

And she lets me – no selfish stroking, no biting my unprotected neck, no shuffling or suggesting another flute of sekt. She lies behind me – long, smooth and still.

I suck in a breath – smelling her sweet sheets. Wonder how long I had forgotten to breathe. Gradually, gradually, I savour this astonishing dimension, slowing right down, stretching out and out...allowing myself to have this.

And that's the revelation. This tender gentleness. This new me. This relaxed and relaxing quality of touch that I have discovered in myself – it allows orgasms in. I didn't even tense up in the throes – didn't have the throes. Making love no longer a fight with myself – with her. Life – no longer quite such a fight.

Father and Sons

James Nash

I was on my knees looking into a dusty case full of chipped glasses and decanters when I saw them. Two oriental figures of boys, perhaps carved out of a dark wood, were sitting, small and round, at the front of a shelf. I picked up the larger of the two. Just as I did so, random sunlight from an upper window struck through him and stained the tips of my fingers pink. The figure, his arms full of a huge carp, was actually carved from a translucent, morello cherry-coloured resin. Red amber from ancient Chinese pine forests. Another hand reached past me into the case picking up the smaller boy.

It made me jump. I got up and turned stiffly. In the half-light of the shop I saw that a young man was already holding his boy high up to the light of the window, as if inviting the sunshine through. And the Chinese figure, holding a small dragon closely to his chest, glowed from within like a ruby, his face a blush of happiness. The young man looked delightedly at the rose colour on his skin, and said, 'Look at that.'

He could have been talking to himself, but then he smiled over at me.

'Hi,' he said.

I smiled back tentatively, as he lowered the figure, weighing it in his hand like a cricket ball. I could barely make out his features in the gloom, just the white of his teeth, the arch of eyebrows, as I tested the weight of the little boy in my hand. He was not heavy.

And then I held my Chinese boy above my head too, up to the

sharp wintry sun glancing through the high window. Motes of dust hung in the air, slowly turning light streamed around him and through him. And I discovered that, apparently smooth-skinned and perfect on the outside, he was, when fully lit, a maze of internal cracks and fissures. The light glinted and was diverted by each fracture, so that it sprang from his knee and his shoulder; and the inside of his head seemed to contain a cobweb of fault lines, of blood vessels. He had perhaps been dropped, or thrown. One, or several, careless owners. Or it may have been the way the amber had formed itself. But it seemed to me that his eyes twinkled. And his face wore the same good-humoured expression as his brother's.

'Aren't they great?' he said, proffering the figure in his hand. I smiled assent but still did not speak. I was bothered by him, by his friendliness, his wanting to engage. But more than that: a familiarity about him. His shape in the half-light of the stall. The way he stood.

I reached out and took it, still warm, from him, and put the brothers together on top of the case. I had once collected small pieces like these, and had long since lost interest, but these two brought out unexpected parental feelings in me. They needed a home. Although priced separately, they belonged together. And I knew that, if I left them in the shop, thoughts of them would be buzzing in my head for days. And that if I went back later in the week they might be gone. Holding them both in one hand, I moved over to the counter in the window, where a young woman was reading a paperback copy of *Oliver Twist*.

The young man, just behind me, said, 'Are you going to buy them?'

'Yes. Love at first sight I'm afraid. They were originally wedding gifts, and are supposed to bring good luck, longevity and fertility. So cheap at the price.'

The shop assistant looked up briefly at this, saw nothing beyond two men chatting, very quickly lost interest and returned to her book.

I looked at him. And in the better light saw him properly for the first time. A shock of recognition, of painful delight, before the chilly realisation ultimately that this was not, and could not be, Simon. Because Simon was dead. Perhaps I looked at him a second or two longer than was usual. But he was not disconcerted, he simply smiled, as if it was his due, and extended one hand. His left one. The other he was using to lean against the counter.

'Hi, I'm Brendan.'

And I realised that his voice was quite different from Simon's, deeper, with a north east inflection. Our hands met and clasped in a handshake. There was no tingle of recognition in the physical meeting. Simon was dead.

We both spoke at the same time.

'I'm a bit short of cash at the moment, otherwise I would have grabbed them from you,' he paused before continuing, 'I've just started a new job.'

'This will be the first thing I've bought for myself for a long time.'

I handed the two figures over to the assistant, trying not to stare at Brendan. But when I looked at him an involuntary smile broke out on my face. He had wandered off and was looking at a collection of tankards. A bit broader in the shoulder. Hair less ginger and more conker-coloured. A similar walk but not the same. I paid for the Chinese figures and had them wrapped, and we walked out of Waterloo Antiques together, onto the little cobbled street at the back of the Corn Exchange.

Now I had a carrier bag in addition to my briefcase. Brendan looked at me, with a kind of hunger. I searched his face for more of Simon. It seemed we both did not want to break the connection we had made. Whatever it was.

'What are you up to now?' he said roughly. Perhaps embarrassment.

'Off to pick up my car. I've parked it down by the brewery.'

'I'll walk a little way with you, if I may.'

I couldn't think of a way of dissuading him. And wasn't entirely sure that I wanted to.

Brendan chatted, and I listened, as we threaded our way under a railway bridge and into the waterfront area. He was twenty-three and had finished university eighteen months before. He was from Middlesbrough. He had recently broken up with his girlfriend. He had never known his mother, been brought up by his dad, and then, at seven when his father had died, had been fostered or been in care throughout the rest of his childhood.

We found ourselves standing on the narrow footbridge over the river to the Tetley's brewery. All around us were the beginnings of new buildings, of a new Leeds. Cranes hung against the now clouded white sky, like crossed swords on an heraldic device. I told him about myself. A surprising amount. His eyes seemed fixed on the river below, but every now and again I felt his gaze on my profile like a warm breath. I was in my mid-forties. Fresh out of a marriage. Senior Social Worker. Fucked up. A father.

'All the 'fs' then,' was his response to this.

I smiled and continued. Two sons. The elder, Simon, had died in a car accident two years before. But I didn't say how much I missed him every single day. How much he would have liked the Chinese figures too. Liked them, as I did, for the way they looked and what they represented. One perfect and the other so mysteriously damaged. Or how much Brendan looked like him, and how fascinating and painful that was. Like picking at a scab obsessively, a day or so too early, and finding you've made yourself bleed. Instead I talked about Oliver who was twelve and lived with his mother. My comic, and strong-minded, youngest son. And curiously it was the first time I had been able to talk about either of the boys without something catching in my voice. Finally I felt I had to justify talking about Simon, and a flash of something brief but unrecognisable passed over Brendan's face when I said, 'Of course the strange thing is that although Simon's dead, I always have to mention him. The fact that I had two sons. Anything else would be betrayal.'

'How old was he, your son?' he asked.

'He was about to be twenty-one,' I answered, looking into the dark and still water below, 'Driving home from university in my wife's car, he just went off the road. The doctors said it could have been a stroke. Our marriage didn't last long after that.'

I felt again the shame I always had when I talked about my marriage break-up. The sense of public failure.

There was a pause, and I could see him assimilating this information, his brows knotted. He was not handsome, just had the pleasant looks of youth. But there was a charm beyond the ordinary in the movement of his face. His willingness to engage. His intelligence. I felt myself very drawn to him, but unwillingly. It felt disloyal to Simon. Close to treachery. And Simon, I had to remind myself, had been intensely shy; he would never have struck up a conversation with a stranger, and indeed would never have been able to meet a stranger's eye.

Steam from the brewery bubbled into the sky behind his head as he said, 'Just the same age as me then.'

I looked at Brendan. He had winded me. And it was as if I was gasping for breath. Surely he knew the effect his words would have? His expression was fascinated, like a scientist who, having discovered a process to measure pain, was trying it out. I turned away from him to look back at the Parish Church. And over to the right at The Royal Armouries like a huge grain silo. The pause pooled into a longer silence.

'Are things any better now?' he finally asked, screwing up his eyes against the sun.

I filled my lungs with air. Regarded him warily. And I talked about my good relationship with my younger son. A nice place to live in Chapel Allerton. A job I enjoyed. In the last few months a girlfriend. A close circle of friends. At the mention of friends, Brendan's brown eyes almost disappeared as he screwed them up in apparent discomfort. He said in a rush, as if embarrassed, 'When I finished university I decided that I didn't want to keep the friends I had made then, so I just stopped seeing them. It felt great making a new start. They were beginning to hold me back.'

He stretched out his hands, palms up, to the water and the Leeds skyline as if in unconscious supplication. Or atonement. An overblown gesture. And I noticed the palm of his right hand had a large, raised red scar across it, like a starfish. It ran from his wrist to the base of his fingers, and from his thumb to the outside edge of his hand. Not new, it must have been a terrible wound. Now it was a huge, bumpy callous. He would be hard put to make a fist with that hand. Or hold a pen.

'What's that?' I said, social worker's antennae alert. He brought his palm up to his chest as if interrogating the scar for a moment. Then he looked at me, holding his hand out to show me. Asking me to share. As if he were five and had got grit in the flesh of his hand. Or a splinter.

'It was when I was in a children's home. The third or fourth one, can't remember which. My gran had just died, my dad's mother, and I kicked off in the kitchen. Went a bit wild, throwing stuff and yelling. I was supposed to be helping serving up one of the meals. One of the care-workers grabbed me and pressed my hand down onto a hot gas ring. Afterwards he swore it was an accident. I suppose I'm lucky it wasn't lit at the time.'

Something in these statements did not ring quite true. Alerted me. I had heard many such stories. Was it the amount of information I was being given? Or the sense that what he had said had been edited for public consumption? I looked at his face for more clues. It was hard to imagine damage below the charming surface. His eyes met mine guilelessly. More green than the blue that my sons and I had shared, along with our uncompromisingly red hair. He nodded his head a few times as if to confirm the horror of it all.

After that there was not much to say. I hefted my briefcase and the carrier bag from hand to hand. We said some awkward goodbyes. Me hoping he would not ask for a telephone number, because for some reason which I had not yet examined, I would have had to refuse. But all he said was, 'Perhaps I can come and visit the Chinese figures in your house, sometime?'

I shook his hand silently and smiled non-committally. He set off back across the bridge to town, and I started walking over to Hunslet, where my car was parked. I turned just once and watched him. And it was like seeing Simon walking off. And for a few seconds, blinded with unshed tears, I relived the loss of him. All my sorrow was as fresh as when I had first experienced it. And I said aloud to the city skyline he had never seen, 'If only I could see you again.'

***

I suppose I was not surprised to come across Brendan some months later. I was sitting in a Chinese restaurant on Vicar Lane

49

with my youngest son Oliver. It was Sunday lunch. One of the fixed parts of my week, when Oliver and I spent an hour or so together. His mother usually devoted Sunday afternoon to marking and preparation as an English teacher at a local high school.

Oliver shovelled huge portions of vegetables into his mouth, head low down over his plate, like a police helicopter, not wanting to miss anything. He was talking with brutal frankness about one of his teachers and was describing both his inability to keep order and the size of his backside, as if both characteristics were contingent on each other. I was laughing. Suddenly he paused in mid-shovel, 'Hey Dad, there's a bloke waving at you from over there.'

I turned and there was Brendan sitting with a middle-aged man on a table opposite us. He waved cheerily at me and grinned over at us. The man he was with smiled politely. He was not having a good time; he just stirred food on his plate with a fork. It was as if my being there, and recognised so cheerily by Brendan, had added to his unease. He said something to Brendan which made him jerk his head like a horse resisting a rider's direction. And at this response the man looked cross and defeated. And out of his depth.

Oliver and I chatted, as I tried to stifle my discomfort. Nevertheless as before I found myself unable to stop looking at Brendan. He had lost weight since I had seen him last and appeared less boy-like. His hair was gelled and was darker than before. An adult was emerging from the roundness of youth. I could see him attempting to soothe his companion down with a great deal of skill. Patting his hand and talking low and fast. The man laughed reluctantly, and looked over at me. There was a look of scorn, or was it pity on his face. What had Brendan said about me? And why did I think it was probably derogatory? Oliver listened intently as I explained where I had met Brendan. How together we'd looked at the Chinese figures now sitting on a window sill in my house. Somewhere near the end of my tale, Oliver could contain himself no longer and burst out, mouth lamentably full, 'But Dad, he looks just like...'

I didn't let him finish, just got up and mumbling something, went off to wash my hands of grease from the spare ribs. Knowing what Oliver had been going to say made the similarities between Brendan and Simon more real and more painful to me. I wanted to run away, taking Oliver with me. Protect ourselves from more hurt, from more reminders.

Coming back, I was jolted to see Oliver in conversation with a young man. They were sitting next to each other. While I was washing my hands, Brendan had left his table and come over to ours. Oliver was laughing delightedly, again mouth open and full of food. Then he seemed to ask a question because Brendan paused momentarily and held his right hand, palm upwards, for Oliver to look at it.

Neither heard my soundless approach over the thick pile of the carpet. I was in time to hear Brendan say, 'Yes, it was a lucky escape. I was in a car accident, and I cut my hand breaking the glass to get out.'

Oliver's eyes went big and round with the answer. I could see him processing this information, and relating it to the death of his elder brother. Brendan didn't miss a beat as he felt my presence behind him.

'Hi,' he said, extending his left hand, 'How are you doing? I just introduced myself to Oliver.'

I found anger and fear welling up inside me. His eyes looked at me innocently. Close to, skin fresh and pink, he looked little older than Oliver. Anybody seeing them together would have no doubt that they shared the same genes. Oliver cried out with enthusiasm,

'Hey Dad, Brendan's been telling me a great story.'

I forced some control into my voice. It came out more or less normally when I said, 'Hello Brendan, nice to see you again. What's happened to your friend?'

Brendan looked momentarily confused. The table where the middle-aged man had been sitting with him was now empty. He gathered himself a little. It was as if he had already forgotten him. With an effort of memory he said, 'Oh him. I've only known him a month. One of those things. What a lucky chance to see you two.'

And he beamed at Oliver, who beamed back with unaffected liking. With a pang I realised that he was responding to Brendan in the same way that I had on our first meeting. Oliver had missed Simon too. And I had never really acknowledged that.

Somehow I eased my son out of the restaurant and into the car, speedily, yet with a controlled politeness.

Brendan knew what I was doing, and why. He stood in the entrance and looked at me, hurrying away and trying not to show my panic. And loss moved slowly down his features emptying them out. Expressionless finally, he had somehow become seven years old. His face was pinched and he was without charm. The face from an old sepia photograph of orphanage children. Only his eyes said anything. The eyes of someone who had been rejected many times before, they had no shine. They said 'Again'.

He raised one hand, when Oliver waved madly at him.

'He's great,' said Oliver. 'Will we see him sometime soon?'

'I'm sure we will,' I replied.

But actually it wasn't until quite a few years later that I saw Brendan next. I was in Leeds City Station, at the end of the university term, waiting for Oliver to appear off the Newcastle train. Through the windows I could see the skyline of a newer, bigger Leeds. Everything had changed so much.

Then I spotted Brendan, coming down an escalator. He was with a man in his late forties. They were standing close to each other, almost touching. It seemed likely they had just met, for Brendan was looking at his new friend speculatively, almost hungrily. As if the man might hold the final pieces of a puzzle for him.

I braced myself unconsciously, although I knew that I was probably immune to him now.

He must have felt my stare because he glanced down and saw me, his eyes meeting and holding mine momentarily. Confusion and remembering fought in his expression briefly. Then from just behind, Oliver's bright head suddenly towered above the throng, and bore past them. He waved at me cheerily, shoving down through the people on the escalator without a second glance around him. My eye contact with Brendan was broken, just as the sun reached through the transparent roof sidings and high windows of the station. I was dazzled. My eyes filled with protective tears. Brendan was in a shimmer of illumination. And for one second, before I was completely blinded, it seemed that the sun shone through him in a shattered network of light. Just like the Chinese boy. Smooth externally, but quite broken inside.

When I blinked and rubbed my eyes, he had gone and Oliver was striding towards me.

I looked at my son with a mixture of relief and love. This was enough.

Statue
Tajinder Singh Hayer

The statue first appeared in the square during May. He set himself beneath the council offices on an upturned milk crate, and laid a cardboard sign at his feet ('Pygmalion's statue' it said), and then waited. That was almost all that he did.

And, for that month, significant interest arose in the shoppers and office-dwellers. His intrusion into the neat (and not so neat) space of the city centre fascinated them; his presence was seen as a pleasing sign of metropolitan growth, and, as though to appease the gods of economic and cultural prosperity, they would drop coins into the tray by his feet, expecting a shift in his posture. Then they would wait. And wait. And the change would come, but at such a rate and at such a time that the paying client had invariably returned to shopping or working.

So it was that the attraction of the statue dulled as the weeks passed, as summer began to screw slowly tighter. It became harder to stop and stare as the buses pushed heat through the city centre; harder to stand and wait as the crowds of others urged movement, as feet began to throb. So the statue was forgotten; his presence smoothed out of difference and into familiarity. He became a true ornament like the ignored reliefs of the city hall.

But Jasvir did not forget. There was something that would not let her, something that impelled her to look out over the square and to the man on the crate; that directed her eyes to the window during meetings, seminars and training exercises. She wondered if it was his clothing, which, although always the same pair of blue shirt and blue trousers, was never unclean or worn. Or perhaps she watched for the changes that came long after the paying viewers had gone; the gentle shift of his limbs as he became an ancient hero struggling with a Gorgon, became David, became an older and more dignified Cupid. Whichever image he adopted, it would be held for hours (sometimes a whole day would pass without him moving). And Jasvir was always there, watching his slow semaphore from above.

Today there was little difference. The only new thing was a group of builders, stripped to the waist, laying out concrete in the square. Jasvir avoided looking at them and focused instead on her statue. He was standing directly beneath the office window, spearing at imaginary fish. He hadn't caught anything since the morning. She willed someone, even those joking, jostling builders, to drop a coin in the tray and free him from his shape. But no-one did. A few tourists idly clicked their cameras and walked away. That was all.

All and the heat. The hottest day of the summer so far, with everything that wasn't metal or concrete wilting in the sun. People hurried to air-conditioned offices and stores. They beaked at their cold drinks and melting ice creams, hoping that the remaining hours would coolly slip away. Even the drunks had moved out of the square (the sun working with more efficiency and severity than the police force). Yet the statue remained as he always was – sure and calm in his immobility. Frozen. Even his sweat obeyed him.

'I hate that scrounger. Do-nothing – that's all he is. Someone should move him. Someone from the Council.'

Jasvir looked across at Ryan, newly arrived from a too-short break, and contemplated a response. He – despite the suit, despite the desk, despite the blond highlights – was not her superior. He was officially an equal in another department, which just happened to be based in the same room as hers. This did not make him superior. She was entitled to her response.

'We *are* from the Council.'

'What?' A film of bafflement slid over his face; he tried to wipe it away with a handkerchief – failed – then looked for water, but the cooler was empty. He moved back to the window, then to his chair and hid, discreetly, behind his desk. The sweat from the run had permeated his suit, turning it into an ill-fitting second skin that embarrassed his skeleton. Jasvir looked at him and thought how much more natural perspiration appeared on the builders, how it seemed to glide from their bodies whilst it hung grimly to this officeman's shape. She watched, but then saw that it was all the same. Sweat – the work of bodies just trying to stay alive on a hot day.

And Jasvir was no different; a realisation she found more shocking than it should have been. It made her aware of the embarrassing moisture that lined her armpits; the sweat that gathered on her lip, accentuating her light hair into a dewy moustache. And that other part. She hid it from Ryan, who sat opposite and ready for the cruel joke. Hid from Ryan and his kind. She shrank from the small green room they shared.

At such times, work became a welcome distraction. She would immerse herself in figures and projections: litter collection rotas, correspondence, funding applications, charity events – the miscellany of local governance. And the place names – Bingley, Saltaire, Manningham – that reassured her so with their familiarity. Or, if she couldn't work, she would take an apple from her bag and cut it neatly in half, then admire the two perfect hearts she had made.

But all this today had to contend with the heat, in which words melted before her eyes, in which apples became unpleasantly sticky, and places became absurdly local and prosaic.

'We could do with air-conditioning in here don't you think?' said Ryan. He was playing with a carton of sour milk at his desk; sniffing it then pulling a face, and then sniffing again. Eventually he would put it down.

'It's not environmentally friendly.'

'So?'

'We're supposed to be an eco-friendly council.'

'Fuck eco, what about us?'

'Yes, but what goes around comes around. You have to appreciate that.'

Nothing. No response at all. An almost utter blankness, and another sniff of the carton. Jasvir wanted to shake him.

'Look. I'll try to explain. We use air-conditioning and we add to global warming; we add to global warming and it gets hotter. That's the way it goes. So better just grin and bear it.'

She said this and thought of how Ryan would be holidaying in the Mediterranean later that summer, of how he would be lapping up the sun without complaint. Browning up and getting drunk. The only place she had ever been to was India; three times to that same village in the north-west. And the pang of jealousy disturbed her. She blinked and saw again the blankness on Ryan; his sheer disregard for anything other than himself, his senses, his...

Jasvir's mobile phone danced across the tabletop. It brought her back.

'That from lover boy?' Ryan smirked. 'You'll be getting fixed up soon.'

Nobody was supposed to know about Pavan. Ryan's awareness was the result of a chance meeting; unfortunate and embarrassing. He used his knowledge to make her squirm occasionally; dance to his little tunes (he knew the differences between them and how they could be exploited – the rumours, the whiff of scandal, anything). Jasvir wished she had a weapon to fight back with – something to spike him as he spiked her – but she didn't. She was facing his opaqueness again. So she hid the phone in her bag with the message unchecked.

Lover boy. Neither word was exactly accurate. Pavan was not a boy he was a man, and he was Jasvir's friend (her mind rejected the word 'boy-friend' or 'man-friend'). Yet, they had been going out together. Specifically, they were dating in that nineteenth-century way that young Punjabi couples have: with secret meetings that feed a self-reciprocating illicitness to their relationship; with public shows of affection either rationed or encrypted; with an awareness of the vast net of social and familial responsibility. 'Boy-friend', 'dating' and 'going out' did not seem apt definitions for the situation.

And *lover.* Love presented other difficulties. It was an emotional state that Jasvir found difficult to categorise. She had expected it to pierce her like an arrow and transform her small, green world. It would be a finding of her other half that would make even the garish spectacles of Bollywood - the lame campness of the men, actresses barely containing their hearts in their chests – seem plausible. All those legends too: Romeo and Juliet; Rama and Sita; Hero and Leander. *That* was love.

But Jasvir's relationship with Pavan held none of these great passions. Instead, what sometimes struck her was the convenience of it; how fitting it seemed. Pavan was a Sikh, young, the right caste, a successful businessman – nothing that her family might object to. In fact, he was a candidate they might have selected themselves. It only seemed that, by hiding their affair, the two of them were simply creating the illusion of a free choice being made. And this thought would have disturbed her (had she allowed it to grow), but she willed it back just as she willed her love forward. She was sure there was something growing there; a budding romance taking its first stiff steps. It was not numbness. It was not numbness...

Jasvir fidgeted in her seat, trying to rub the pins and needles from her legs. It had been three hours now, and three more remained until the end of the working day. Her leather chair was uncomfortable in the warmth and streaky with moisture; the work on her table was being looked over rather than done; and Ryan was prowling the office. Both their tempers were stretched.

Periodically, he would leave the room without an excuse. He would be gone for ten minutes and return less exasperated – calm almost – until he walked to the water cooler; then he would become angry again when he saw it was empty. This cycle continued well into the afternoon until the support staff came with a new container. Then Ryan was forced to look for a new distraction. He found it, three hours before the end of the day, beneath the window. A rare moment of inspiration.

Below, the statue was still holding his spear pose. He still held it, though juddered a little, when the milk carton crashed down onto his left arm. The contents missed most of his torso and spilled out over his trousers. The carton rattled to a stop by his feet. There was no-one in the square to watch this piece of vandalism; the builders were on their break and the sun had scoured the rest. Only one other person had seen the incident.

'You threw it,' said Jasvir.

'It was an accident.'

'You threw it.'

'Why would I throw it, Jas?'

The answer was 'why not?'. She had seen it on his face as he had looked out over the statue, as he had raised the carton to eye level and pretended to read the advertising; a rare moment when she had pierced into his mentality. And it struck her as before; the sheer casualness of his actions. There were no repercussions in his world. A dropped carton stayed dropped. Jasvir had felt him make the choice, seen him pretend to fumble, and protested too late. She had *waited* for a reason to protest. She had wanted a reason.

'He might appreciate the shower,' smiled Ryan, then lost that painful smirk a little as he returned to his desk. His duties still lay there, unfinished, and there were still three hours to go.

'You should apologise. It's not right,' said Jasvir trying to focus her anger into one moral push. She had hoped for something stronger.

Ryan lifted a sheet of paper and talked underneath it. 'I'll do it later.'

It was no use. Jasvir hadn't the stamina to hate him; not now and not forever. His continued presence only triggered bouts of dislike, not a festering anger. Had Ryan been a stranger, she would have passed him without any emotion. Had Ryan been a colleague elsewhere, she would have made polite small-talk with him. But there, in that room together, they traded their occasional barbs; it would never go beyond that. Jasvir recognised the unfortunate uniqueness of their relationship (its artificiality as well). She felt that somewhere beneath that exterior was a reasonable man, just married and with a new home, who had been pushed by heat and boredom into petulance. Still, she couldn't help feeling that, for him, it was nothing a night out in Leeds or Manchester wouldn't fix. There were some prejudices she would not drop.

But as she looked out of the window she realised that her hate, like her love, was a lukewarm emotion; both would reach the same mundane sourness. They would never rise to any great heights for long. They were not searing. They were not solid or immovable.

They were not overpowering legends that people would write songs about. They were not… And then she saw her statue again. The milk still dripped a little from his body (already rancid, it would stink even more as the open air got to it). But he had not moved. He still held his heroic posture no matter what was thrown at him. A body that said *'just grin and bear it'*.

Jasvir could have smiled, but she just watched. Then she returned to her duties.

Three hours later, and she was downstairs, draping an unnecessary jacket over her arm and waving goodbye to the security staff as she left. Left into a day that was beginning to surrender around her. The builders had packed away their equipment, leaving their work half-completed, and all the other office-workers had gone. Shop fronts were closing their metal eyelids. And the light was starting to brown – like a left apple core.

Usually, this was her favourite part of the day. It was as though she had left the furnace of her office, and could revel in the almost orgasmic coolness of outdoors. There was no-one to watch her and there was a pleasant stillness at the heart of the city. The magic of things winding down.

But again she saw her statue, looking more solitary than ever in the deserted square. And this was not usual. Normally, he would find a chance to ghost away in the evening. She would be absent from her desk for a minute, and he would take his opportunity to disappear; it was as though he was watching *her* (impossible though it seemed) for a sign of movement. Yet, now he had broken their routine (the game in which Jasvir had made herself complicit). He was still there. *Still and still.*

Jasvir contemplated moving towards him and perhaps saying something, but that would be another rule broken. In all the months that he had been in the square, she had hurried past and avoided looking in his direction. She had never dropped anything in the tray (she didn't know why) and had never got truly close to him. All her viewing was done from above. There had been no communication between them.

But now, as she moved nearer, she could see the things she had missed from a distance or in her shuffling quickness to get to work. See, for example, that his tanned skin obscured both his race and his age; she could tell nothing from his features (in fact, they seemed to change greatly as she came closer or as she altered her view). He could have stood in any city in any country and passed as an almost-native. Jasvir tried to imagine it; all the parts of the world that had hurried around him whilst he had watched in absolute stillness. Absolute because she had never seen him blink.

She came as close to him as she had ever done before (no more than a few metres separated them) and then felt the surge: the point-of-no-return. The possibilities flooded through her mind: maybe she was in love, maybe this statue *was* love, maybe love was not innate, maybe love was a shaped, worked thing, maybe love… maybe…

She needed an excuse to talk to him (something he could not ignore), and then she saw the milk stains still on his clothing. Even the carton remained by his feet. Then Jasvir knew that she would apologise for Ryan, and that that apology would spread out, encompassing the builders and the disinterested tourists and the shoppers and the cruel city beyond. She would say sorry on behalf of everything.

But her words only limped out. 'Excuse me, my name is Jasvir Kaur. I work in the offices behind you, on the second floor, and I…' They were not enough. They were trapped in politeness. She could not say…

And then he moved. It was unnoticeable at first, but there was a definite shift; like the change between seasons, like something coming to life. But it was a slow movement, made with difficulty as though a great weight was upon him; the overpowering gravity of a hot day.

And Jasvir stepped forward too with great difficulty, because she could see what he was doing. The statue had dropped his imaginary lance and was twisting to face her. When his actions were becoming absolutely clear, she stopped. Because, before her, he gently opened out his arms and invited an embrace. Then his mouth spread out into a practised, beatific smile. His eyes switched on. It seemed as though his whole being was changing for her, was channelling the sun's power, and was trying to pull her in with the force of its pleading.

But Jasvir did not run towards him. Neither did she smile or embrace in return. She was paralysed. All she could do was stand. Still. And watch. And watch. And let the concrete continue setting around her ankles.

Percentages
Steve Dearden

Helen slams her briefcase on to the kitchen table, slaps down the court order for the unpaid council tax. 'Jenny -'

'I'm sorry Helen, I've just not had -'

'Then run a city Jenny. You say you haven't had time to pay the city, try running it.'

An unpaid bill is not what I need to talk about.

'No Helen, look -'

'You know what I've been having meetings about all afternoon? Chewing gum. I thought we were supposed to manage the serious stuff: cars, acids, asbestos. Today? Chewing gum. The city's paved with it.'

'H-'

'Then drain covers: people suing us because they've been -'

I have something to tell Helen. 'I -'

'Now we have to have a team to check whether-'

I have perfected the art of listening just enough to say 'Yes' occasionally, 'No' in the right place, to bob my head, purse my lips attentively while thinking about the things I would say if Helen let me get a word in. But tonight I'm biting my thumb knuckle and wondering if Cyd will keep in touch.

Cyd's one of our banking assistants, coasting between her degree and working out what it is she wants to do with the rest of her life. She's the brightest brain in the branch. On her first morning we discovered we both remembered places by taste rather than scenery or buildings: Cranachan Kilmartin. Hetton dill lamb.

Live cockles in Carnac. Rouen Gewurztraminer, an ice pile of snails, mussels, cockles, oysters, langoustine. Bruges chips with mayonnaise. St Petersburg ice cream. Anjuna bel puri, Vancouver bo nhung dam. We both had parents whose sacred texts were Elizabeth David, Claudia Roden, Jane Grigson, so as kids beans on toast, egg and chips were exotic; things you only got at other kid's houses. I looked forward to family camping holidays: Angel Delight, Fray Bentos pies, Chunky Chicken.

Cyd says 'Fray Bentos? Chunky Chicken?' like she's turning over bits of wreckage. I haven't dared tell her the menu of the first restaurant where I worked in the seventies: prawn cocktails, whitebait, melon with an orange slice and a cherry on sticks, steak diannes, trout and almonds, ice creams, fruit salad meringue for pud. And I have not told Helen how I watch for Cyd putting her pens in her pot, closing down her computer, how 'accidental' meetings on the way to the station have become a drink most nights.

Helen's well into her unloading, now it's all the things being the Chief Exec of a city means she's responsible for, market traders, teachers, taxis, paedophiles, rivers, soil, 'we're even policing the bloody air now.'

One time, standing in the packed carriage home, I was telling Cyd how all those family holidays - the tents, campsites, lakes, forests, beaches, towns - all blend into a memory of sticky car seats on the back of hot legs, a scratchy impatience in the small of my back.

She said 'A scratchy impatience in the small of your back?'

In the Arts Bar once I was telling her about my first job in a real restaurant, how I loved the way we ordered, took delivery, gathered, turned out, prepared, arranged taste, colour, shape, sent plates out on a waiter's arm into the buzz of covers.

She said 'The buzz of covers?' Her smile like hot breath on my arm.

Another time, in one of those bars where the kitchen seems three floors or even blocks away and the menu is a slim card and the waitress all about drinks, Cyd asked me why I had left restaurants to work in a bank. I was shouting against the sound system, shredding my voice, my lips on her ear 'Realised...that kinda life...slavery...too many hours...too hot...grind. Loved it...but.' I held up my hand. 'Burnt too bad to grip...look.' Did the finger yap yap talking thing that shows how I still can't close my palm even after twenty years. 'The owner then...wonderful man...gave me a chance...kept me on...taught me the books.'

Cyd holds my hand, prods the scar tissue with her thumb.

On the train later, sitting at Platform 2a waiting for a crew. 'That guy taught me to see the bumps and holes in budgets, cashflows.'

'So?'

'So I went into banking, specialised in restaurant, bar accounts, people moved their accounts because of me, it was fantastic, I was one of them. I could make the bank work for them.'

'Could?'

'Yes could. In a way that I can't now.'

Cyd said 'The trouble with you love, is everything you say's in the past tense.' *A scratchy impatience in the small of your back. A buzz of covers. Everything you say is in the past tense.* I love the way Cyd says things in a way that means afterwards I have to shake out our conversations and, opening my fingers slightly, blow in my palm.

'Are you listening to me?' Helen gets a Sauvignon from the fridge. 'Today Prescott's office told me that by next Tuesday. Next. Tuesday. They want a policy on how we manage seven hundred and fifteen thousand people's weight.'

I would like to reach Helen, to stop her flow. She holds the unopened wine in one hand, her forehead in the other. 'This morning – an absurd investment seminar for Thai business men, I was thinking *fuck, I even have a foreign policy now.*'

I take the bottle, find the corkscrew, try to tune out but only half succeed, she's on about, 'support…support…support… support…support' stuff about business, pregnancy, refugees, employment. I pour her wine. 'We support so much I feel like the scaffolding you see packed into gutted buildings holding up the fronts: brain support.'

'I have something I have –'

'This lunch time I got back to the office to find I'm two Heads of Service down. Two, not three this week, so it's an improvement.'

Helen has finished her wine already. I refill the deep glass that if she is not careful her grip will shatter. I want to tell her how today my boss Tony said, 'I'm taking you for a drink.' Not like, *would you like a drink*, or *you need a drink*, or *I'd like to buy you a drink*, but like *we need to talk*. Or more like *you need a talking to.*

Tony is all skinny wrists and fingers, he probably has an intricate relationship with his flannel but is powerful now the bank has *refocused*. He says things like *let me ask you this* before telling you. Says before he lies to me *let me look you in the eye and say*, 'I don't want to lose you, account holders rate you highly…' pulls his cuffs as if he is arming them, '…but I am beginning to wonder whether you'd rather be on their payroll than ours.'

I say 'Customers.'

'Yeh yeh.'

'Customers not account holders.'

He had come to observe me meeting one of my oldest customers – and as soon as we were on the street afterwards, Tony was waving his bony little hands. 'I can't believe you talked so much about bars and restaurants and so little about banking. I have to say this to you Jen, your targets are not about how popular you are, but new accounts and getting existings to switch to Business First, Premier Plus. You offered him a loan on his existing account!'

'It's the cheapest way for him to borrow.'

He said 'I'm taking you for a drink.' Then later in the Arts 'I expect you're dry white,' and although that was actually what I wanted I said 'No, red'. So he ordered two small reds, chose a table at the end of the bar, laced his knuckles 'I want to say this in a way that we will both understand. There is no room on my team for people who don't give a hundred and ten per cent.'

When the waitress brought our wine he thanked her like she had handed him a thin knife with which to stab himself in the throat. 'Look I am sure HR have solutions for this kind of thing, but we don't have the time they seem to need to do anything these days, we're already six months into the year and your targets haven't left base so either we see marked improvement right away or we talk about…I dunno, you could redeploy but not at this level.' He had already taken away most of the things that made me love my job, I couldn't bear hearing him take away the job itself, his mouth moving like the corners of words stung his lips.

I thought just for a second about putting my side - the value of my relationships with customers – trust - how they confide in me more than they should a bank manager, admit their dreams. But all I could think of was how I see, how I taste this city in a way Tony never will - while he sleeps the suppliers who bank with me take carcasses, strip, bone, joint, tie, they simmer trimmings to stocks, bake, pipe, mould, and while Tony sits in his nose-to-tailed rush-hour Jag, deliveries are well underway, veg, fish, fruit, wines through the morning, then the first customers, some before places are quite set up, in from shopping, out of town, work, people meeting, friends, business, holes in credit cards, change lighter from tips, turfing the last of them out to take stock, restock, send out to replace things there's been a run on, before the evening the staff meal, almost the best cooking of the day, then the early birds through to roosting stragglers and if we're lucky last orders somewhere, placing orders for the next day to the night birds on our mobiles.

Our mobiles? Cyd would say '*Our* mobiles?'

I realised I was sitting looking at Tony how Cyd would have sat back at an angle, pulling her chin. I wanted to lean over and squeeze my fingers under his kneecap. 'What does a hundred and ten per cent mean?'

Tony sat up like I had squeezed him. 'Having everything, not relaxing.'

'A hundred and *ten* per cent? Come on Tony, you're a banker.'

'One ten per cent means are you sure everything really does mean everything? Are you sure your competitor hasn't something you haven't thought of? Are you sure he isn't about to have something that makes your everything not everything?'

'Tony, show me a hundred and ten per cent.'

Tony reached across to the bar for a large empty wine glass, he poured his small red into it, then took my small red, poured that in too. 'You have no wine, you are looking at mine, I have it. Capisco?'

Little Tony saying *capisco* made me laugh, made me want to push a small hole in his forehead with my fingernail, like his little 'o' mouth.

That's when I did it. I need to tell Helen what I did.

'Helen listen, for God's sake listen.'

'I'm sorry love, it's not the council tax, though I am mad about that. You know the press will have me if that comes to anything. Pay it, I'll pay it now, where's the chequebook, look I love my job I love this place but sometimes I just…tonight coming home…'

'It's in the drawer, here.'

'...outside Henry Moore some lad, lager can and roll up shouts "Oi, you're boss of council aren't you, you're always on box 'bout how great Leeds is, what the fuck do you do? What do you do for me, the real Leeds eh?"' Helen does a thing with her mouth that is both crying and looking for how to cry. 'The real Leeds.'

I feel a twist, a glass fleck in the flesh between my forefinger and thumb, a long sliver shock shooting up inside my wrist almost to my elbow, so deep in the scar tissue my palm flexes, connects to my finger ends so I'm not sure whether my hand jumps or pushes, whether I go to slap, strike, scratch, paddle, claw but suddenly we are standing, her mouth open, my mouth open, my hand frozen in the air between us. She knows I have performed a trick, I have thrown something and caught it, made it disappear just before it became a red mark on her cheek, or blood on her lip, a new territory, a place we would need reverse gear. Helen reaches to take hold of the table's edge as if I have struck her, 'I'm sorry, I'm sorry, I'm sorry. Tell me, what is it? I'm sorry - your turn.'

Sometimes in meetings I hear people refer to Helen as *That Helen Charnley*. Say things like *Things have changed for the better since that Helen Charnley arrived*. Or *That Helen Charnley, she's a good thing*. And *We need to get Helen Charnley on board first*. Sometimes people say to me *You live with that Helen Charnley don't you?* I love all the ways they say Helen's name, I love it as much when they like her as when they don't, how she lifts them, how she gets under their skin. I put my arms under her shoulders and hug her onto me wishing, as always, that she could let her sobs out rather than grind her teeth, rock with me rather than jag her head side to side. I say each word slowly, placing them into the distance between me and the woman I am holding in my arms.

'I left the bank. The bank left me.'

'Oh shit.' Helen loosens her hug like she is going to step away and talk about the mortgage, but she doesn't, she seems even taller than usual. 'It's no surprise, I could see it coming. I'm glad you've done it, you needed to.' Although my feet are still on the ground I'm being carried. I know why I love Helen completely and why after the meeting with Tony I ran across town to her office at the Town Hall, for what luckily I realised would have been an absurd entrance into a meeting about waste.

So I rang Cyd, we met in the Fat Cat. Cyd curled her lip. 'So? What happened? There's a suit's summit back at the office.'

I suppose I wanted her to cheer, to be excited, to have a celebration drink at least. I said 'Bet you didn't expect that.'

Cyd sat back, 'What does it matter what I expected?'

So I asked her what she thought and she smiled a tight little flat smile, 'What does it matter what I think?' Not cold, but no hairs on the arm stuff either 'What do *you* think?' Almost as if she was embarrassed for me. 'I have to get back, I'm not like you, they want to know where I am every minute.' On the pavement outside she said, 'Actually I'm leaving a week on Monday, a friend of mine's got a flat in Strasbourg, I don't know what but hey, anyway…' She kissed me on the lips.

I am trying to hold onto the belief that the way Cyd said *What does it matter what I think?* was because she felt indifferent towards banks and careers and jobs, not towards me.

Helen breaks our hug, I tell her 'I broke a one hundred and ten per cent full wine glass across Tony B's nose.'

She looks at me like I work for her, but that feels good. 'You cut him? Hurt him?'

I shrug 'He made a lot of noise, until he realised that wasn't cool.'

'They've had you in?'

'No, tomorrow.'

'Are they involving the police?'

'They haven't decided.'

Helen almost laughs. 'Bloody hell, bad days, you and me both.' She pours herself more wine, opens the kitchen door to let the last of the evening's warm breeze in. 'On the way home I was on the mobile and the conversation got complicated, a legal thing we're having problems with. I turned off so I could stop and concentrate. This guy came over from his front garden and said 'Do you know you shouldn't have turned right? What's the point of the council putting up all those big signs if you're going to ignore them?' I don't know what it was, maybe I was still wound up about that boy outside Henry Moore, but I called him oh, I don't know, f'ings and bastards and…I disgusted myself. As I was saying it I was thinking *Where's this come from? This feels like being out of control.*'

Helen takes my hand, strokes out from the scarring, to my fingertips, up inside my forearm. 'Most of this year you have been so angry, you talk about the bank, about little else. Angry angry angry. I think why does she talk about it all the time if she hates it so much?'

'I loved it.'

'Tonight, me shouting at that guy I thought, shit, I'm becoming Jenny. I'm glad you left, really glad, we'll deal with this. If you like I'll come with you tomorrow. Now cook something. Tell me what happened, the details.'

The Model Woman

Dee Rimbaud

Tony and his brother are debating the finer points of a football match, which was televised and shown in recorded highlights last night after the ten o'clock news. I am nominally included in the conversation as I was there last night while they watched it, in my usual capacity as hostess. When I was not fetching beer or running other errands I sat in my armchair, drinking from a can of Tennants Lager, on which there was a picture of scantily clad woman who made me feel like a frump in comparison. But I am *not* a frump! Tony is always telling me how sexy I am. Not that he paid me much attention last night. Him and Eck had eyes only for the television set; and they turned the air a crimson shade of blue, as they shouted out insults and instructions to the referee and the players. This depressed me and caused me to drink faster than I usually do. It depressed me because of its futility. It's stupid enough to shout at the television as if you had the power of God over events that were going on in a distant place, but to shout at recorded highlights of something that had taken place several hours ago seemed both absurd and infantile.

'That referee hadn't a clue, eh love?' says Tony, directing his attention towards me, trying to enlist my support 'Hateley clearly took a dive before McKimmie came into contact with him. No way was it a penalty.'

'Aw c'mon off of it Tony!' says Eck, before I've a chance to reply, 'Hateley was stretchered off.'

'The Huns are always fucking well pulling off stunts like that,' says Tony with a surprising vehemence. 'Sorry love,' he adds, remembering himself, 'Scuse my Ps and Qs.'

I don't know why he says that, but he always does after he says the F-word or the C-word. I think he thinks I find these words offensive because I don't use them myself. I'm neither here nor there about swear words. I've heard them since the year dot, so I'm used to them. They don't offend me. I don't swear myself because of my upbringing. My mum and dad were both quite pious Catholics and I'd have got hammered if I'd ever sworn.

'Aw c'mon Tony,' says Eck, 'be reasonable!'

'Be reasonable? Be reasonable?' screeches Tony. 'What is it with you? Are you some sort of closet blue-nose or something?'

I look at Eck. Then I look at Tony. Then I look back at Eck. He has a wounded look, like a wee bird that's just been pawed out of the air by a tomcat; and that's what Tony looks like...a big, swaggering, cock-sure tomcat. Tony is always trying to score points off of Eck. I guess it's a sibling thing, but I think he's jealous of Eck as well. Eck still has a full head of hair on him; and he's only Tony's junior by two years. He's also a lot more handsome than Tony.

Last night though, there was little difference between them. The pair of them were like beer-bloated imbeciles. I couldn't bear to look at them: I kept my eyes fixed firmly on the television, even though the match was boring me rigid. I don't know how they found any highlights to put on. I certainly couldn't see any. Even the penalty that Tony and Eck are still arguing about was boring. The goalkeeper dived the wrong way and the ball just sort of rolled into the net. Honestly, I don't know why we bothered watching it at all. We knew beforehand that Aberdeen were beaten one-nil by Rangers: it was on the news. Aside from anything, Tony and Eck are Celtic supporters.

I don't mind so much if it's a Celtic game on the telly, even the recorded highlights: as long as I don't know the score beforehand. I like Celtic because they play in the same colours as Hibs; and being of Irish descent, it's natural that my favourite colour is green. I suppose I've adopted Celtic as my team since moving to Glasgow, but still – if it came down to a match between Celtic and Hibs – I'd support Hibs. I'll always support Hibs. Tony knows this fine and just about tolerates it, but he still slags me every now and then for being a *snooty Edinburgh bird*. I don't know why. There's nothing snooty about the bit of Granton where I come from; and he knows it.

Truth is, I don't really like football that much. I suppose that's not really surprising for a woman, but when I was a kid I loved it with a passion. My dad used to take me to see Hibs play almost every Saturday. Sometimes we'd even travel to Glasgow or Aberdeen or Dundee to see them. I used to like away matches especially. That was back in the early seventies, the glory days. I remember especially winning 7-0 against Hearts in the league; and beating Celtic 5-3 in the Dryburgh Cup final and 2-1 in the League Cup final in the same year. Hibs were a real force to be reckoned with back then. My dad still talks about them days. It was Hibs' finest hour, he says. Now they're so rubbish he doesn't bother going to see them play, not even when they're at home.

I didn't have time for Donny Osmond or the Bay City Rollers back then. My room was a shrine to Hibernian FC; and especially to Joe Harper who was drop dead gorgeous. I cried the day I heard he was leaving Hibs.

It's funny, but I saw him on television recently. He was a guest commentator on Scotsport. I was surprised at how old he looked. He was still vaguely handsome, in an old and haggard sort of way, but what really bothered me was how boring he was. He just kept on saying all these stupid things that footballers say like: '*at the end of the day*' and '*it's a game of two halves*' and '*it's goals that count*', really stupid, mindless things. Any time I hear anyone say '*at the end of the day*' it makes me think of David Coleman and Jimmy Hill; and I feel sick to the pit of my stomach. My dad never talked in clichés. When he talked about football it sounded like poetry. It was his enthusiasm that infected me as a kid. How could I not have ended up loving football?

I mind my dad telling me about Bill Shankly who's famous for saying that football was more important than life. My dad didn't agree with him there, but he admired the spirit of it. He said yon Shankly was a 'true football man'. My dad had a big passion about true football men. There were lots of them back then: people like Jock Stein, Denis Law and Stanley Matthews. At the time, I understood what Shankly meant, but now I think football is mostly boring and depressing. My dad said money destroyed it all. He's right though: how can folk pay five million pounds for a footballer when they can't even find money to keep hospitals open?

Tony and Eck are still arguing about that damn penalty. I only really noticed this because Tony said, 'At the end of the day that penalty cost Aberdeen the game.' It was like a synchronicity or something, him saying that; and it made me feel a wave of nausea, the sort you get after drinking too much the night before. I don't know why, but when Tony says things like that I want to shout at him. A lot of the things he says make my blood boil. Most of the time it's harmless enough things; and I don't know why they upset me so much, but sometimes he can be downright pig-ignorant. Yesterday afternoon at the restaurant, I was *that* close to just packing my bags and leaving him for good.

We were sitting at the staff table, having a fag break after the lunch rush was over. Tony and Eck and their cousin Alfonso were talking about football, as usual. I was sitting, making out I was reading a *Cosmopolitan*, but I was really eavesdropping on a couple sitting at the window table. Sometimes I do that during breaks or after the shift has finished and we're winding down with a beer or a wine or something. This couple were very glamorous-looking. The woman was just like a model out of a magazine. She was wearing a beige check skirt suit, which looked like it had been tailored especially for her. There was a slim, gold bracelet round her wrist; and this seemed to emphasise how slim and elegant she was. It also added a certain sophistication to her every gesture. I watched her carefully, over the top of my magazine. She was very refined: even the way she swept her hair back over her ears to reveal her little mother-of-pearl earrings was refined. Her hair itself was gorgeous: straight out of the Timotei advert; pure blonde, like the colour my hair was before I hit puberty. Her boyfriend was a total dish. They were made for each other. He was wearing a designer label suit; and he looked for all the world like a film actor, like a younger, more handsome version of Robert De Niro. He oozed self-confidence; and his gestures had a nonchalant, dreamy quality; like he was moving through a liquid that was thicker than air, but thinner than water. He was a bit drunk, but unlike Tony or Eck, this only added to his charm. At least, to me: his girlfriend though seemed to be irritated by it. She kept accusing him of not paying attention to what she was saying. Her voice was a bit pinched-sounding. I, on the other hand, was paying her as much attention as was humanely possible. I couldn't hear all that she was saying though because Tony, Eck and Alfonso were having quite an animated conversation. I couldn't hear what her man was saying because he was facing away from me, but his voice had a lovely, soft murmuring quality to it, like the sound of a slow moving river. I was really surprised that his girlfriend was so agitated because I'd have been hypnotised into acquiescence by the sound of his voice alone, never mind his good looks and expensive clothes. His girlfriend though seemed to be getting more and more exasperated with him. Eventually, she shouted at him, loud enough for the whole restaurant to hear. 'Oh for fuck's sake! What's the use?' This caused Tony, Eck and Alfonso to swivel round and gawk at her. The whole restaurant seemed to freeze into silence. Then the woman got up and stormed off into the ladies' toilet. Even in a rage she was elegant. She carried herself with the sort of dignity you only see in the movies. If it had been me I'd have tripped over a chair leg or something and people would be thinking I looked like a right piece of baggage.

After her exit the restaurant came alive with a buzz of excitement. Everybody was speaking in loud whispers, presumably so the woman's boyfriend wouldn't overhear them. I don't think he was much bothered anyway. He signalled the waiter, as cool as you please, gave him some cash and walked out without waiting for the change. He pushed through the smoked glass double doors and walked out onto the pavement in the pouring rain. Almost immediately a cab drew up. He got in and left us to our idle gossip and speculation. That was it, he was gone: not a feather ruffled.

'Right stroppy cow!' hissed Tony.

'Brass neck on her,' agreed Alfonso.

'Telling you,' said Tony, 'if she were mine I'd have belted her one.'

I know it was probably just male bravado, but it really made me angry, him saying that. He didn't know anything about the woman; and already he was deciding she needed putting in her place. I knew it was only words: I knew Tony wouldn't hit anyone, least of all me, but still, I was spitting with rage.

I got up and went to the toilet. I needed to get away from the three of them. I knew I'd say something I'd regret if I didn't. When I got in there, the woman was fixing her make-up in the mirror: looking for all the world like a model from *Cosmopolitan*. I wanted to talk to her, but felt too shy, so I went into the cubicle, sat on the pan and tried to gather my thoughts. Then the tears welled up inside and I started to cry. It was impossible to gather my thoughts: they were all over the place, running riot inside my head. All I could see was that I was destined for a life of misery and drudgery. That if I married Tony I'd just continue working as a waitress until I got pregnant; and then I'd be a housewife; and that would be it. The more I thought about it, the more I thought about just calling the engagement off. I kept thinking about what Tony said he'd have done to the model woman and I couldn't get it out of my head that he might become a wife beater after all. The women's magazines were always warning you about it. I kept thinking about the times he'd put me down or tried to control me; and the more I thought about it, the more it seemed likely. Maybe once he'd got me married and up the spout, once he'd got me over a barrel, his dark side would come out. These doubts made me so miserable I sobbed out loud. I couldn't help myself.

'Are you alright?' said the model woman through the cubicle door. She said it in such a peaches-and-cream voice that I felt safe to confide in her. I unsnibbed the cubicle door and stood up.

'Oh look at you, pet,' she said. 'Your mascara's run.' She led me to the mirror and dabbed away the offending mess with a small facecloth. Then she offered me some of hers. It was in an expensive-looking frosted glass and chrome tube: so unlike the cheap plastic ones I buy from Boots it might as well have come from another planet. I felt its smooth strange textures in my hand and savoured them, thinking that this would be the first and last time I'd ever feel anything as exquisite as this. It caused me to let out another sob. The model woman asked me what was wrong and I just blurted out all my jumbled emotions about Tony, hardly pausing for a breath. She listened patiently, then when I came to a halt she gave me a hug. Then she told me that Tony sounded like a useless waster and I should just dump him. Then she laughed and told me I'd be better off on my own because all men are bastards, one way or another. With that, she breezed out the door in a shining haze of righteous indignation; and I was left alone, feeling like a frump with expensive make-up on.

Once I'd cooled off a bit I went and sat back down beside Tony, Eck and Alfonso. They were still discussing the incident, but had moved along some and were generally agreeing amongst themselves as to what a woman's place should be. They didn't even have the decency to change the topic of the conversation as I joined them, which made me feel a sinking gloom. I was no longer angry, just depressed. I interrupted them to tell them that I was feeling ill and was going home. A look of concern flickered across Tony's face. I quickly told him it was my time of the month as that would ensure no further questions. I wasn't lying really, but I wasn't exactly telling the truth either.

Before leaving, I went off to find Antonio, Tony and Eck's father and our boss. I went into the kitchen and was told that Antonio was last seen checking in a consignment of pinto beans. So I went down the back stair into the gloomy cellar and made my way between piles of netted vegetables and stacks of cans towards the delivery door, all the while being careful not to trip or bang my head on the ceiling. Antonio was standing outside, under a ragged awning, smoking a cigarette and looking thoughtfully up at the grey Glasgow sky. The downpour was over, but it was still drizzling.

'D'you know?' he said to me. 'I still think the rain is beautiful, even after thirty-five years in this country.' He took my hand in his, as he often did; and gave it a little squeeze. I always liked it when he did that. He had big, stubby baker's hands; and holding them made me feel like a little girl again. I liked Antonio a lot. He was like an eccentric, Italian version of my own dad. He had the same kind of turn of phrase. With my dad it was the football. With Antonio it was Italy. Whenever he talked about that magical, far off country he would hold my heart in thrall. He made it sound so romantic and old-time I was just dying to visit it. I'd made Tony promise me that we'd spend our honeymoon there: that he'd take me out on a gondola in Venice and sing me a love song from the opera; and then we'd go and stay in a room with a view in Florence.

'You know something?' said Antonio. 'I used to go out and walk in the rain when I lived in the old country. It didn't rain much in Naples, but when it did I would go out walking until I got soaked to the skin.' He laughed gently to himself. 'You couldn't do that here though, you'd get pneumonia or some such. The old girl, God bless her, she hated the rain. She was always pining for the sun, so she was.' Antonio's eyes got that misty, faraway look as they always did when he talked about his departed wife. Then he gave a wee start, like he'd suddenly come to his senses; and he asked me what it was I wanted. I told him that I was not feeling well; and he told me I should go home and get into bed with a hot-water bottle. He told me that that was what the old girl did when she had her moontime. I was surprised at what he called it. It sounded so otherworldly.

After I got home I went to bed, even though I didn't really feel ill. I took a hot-water bottle as Antonio recommended. Its warmth made me feel good in the half-light of the room. I looked out the window at the driech autumn weather and thought about Antonio standing in the yard, looking at it and loving it; and remembering all about Italy. It made me feel better, just thinking about Antonio.

Then I thought some about how Tony was like Antonio in so many ways. I remembered all the romantic things that he's done for me; and I imagined us getting old together and how he'd be just like his father. Then I didn't feel so bad anymore about all the stupid things he'd said.

Later that evening though, while we watched the football match on the telly, the doubts surfaced again.

Breaking for the Border
Mandy MacFarlane

He'll probably call you up half an hour after you've just met on Boar Lane suggesting a variety of activities for you both to do on your second date. If you're not in, he'll leave a number of messages on your machine with a list of his ideas, which you may at first find a little overpowering.

When you phone him back he will be delighted to hear from you and thank you for calling. He'll sound genuinely enthusiastic when you agree to one of his suggestions. He'll want to come and get you and you will be impressed that the man you are dating has transport and will go to the trouble of picking you up. You'll agree to go jogging in Hyde Park and even though you're not very fit you are very keen to try something different.

He'll come and call for you and then drive you up to the park where you'll spend the next hour in a kind of breathless torture. Afterwards he'll take you back to his house where he'll rustle up some guacamole with lemon and garlic, which no doubt you will be very impressed by. He'll tell you about his trips to Latin America which will suck you in further and then he'll open a bottle of your favourite red wine and you'll think you're in heaven.

His flat which he describes as bijou will have recently been Hoovered and the toilet cleaned. His ornaments, pinecones and shell collection will strike a chord in your subconscious and you will feel strangely at home. His music collection which will coincidentally mimic your own will soften your defences and make you feel foolishly that he is some kind of soulmate.

He will ask you a lot of questions about yourself and in turn will feel compelled to tell you his own life story in one evening. This will be a detailed account of how his marriage broke down and about the numerous games his ex-wife played. He will explain how he was a victim of her instability and her failure to express emotions. You will mistake his confession as a desire to communicate and be understood, but it will actually be part of a greater self-obsession which is nothing to do with you whatsoever.

At this point your best friend Debra will be over the moon for you. She will be relieved that at last you have met a man who is showing you some kind of interest and not afraid to open up like so many others of his ilk, who proved to be vague and elusive. So she'll egg you on and fill your head with all sorts of girlish nonsense which you'll swallow wholeheartedly.

The next time you see each other you will go out in his Citroen 2CV and he will take you to a beautiful part of the North Yorkshire coast. He will have got up early and gone to some trouble to buy another bottle of your favourite Chilean red, French bread and camembert. You will walk hand-in-hand along the shore and he will let slip that this is not the first time he has walked here. You will not be alarmed as you are having such a nice time and you are grateful to him for getting you out of the city. You will confidently think that it won't turn sour for you like it has with how many others?

You will go back to his car and he will make tea on a gas stove and roll you a cigarette. You will sit back in the sunshine and count your lucky stars.

On the road home he will suggest stopping for a drink which you will agree to. He will down a couple of pints in the quarter-of-an-hour before last orders. You will be slightly taken aback at this, as everything else during the day will have been so leisurely. But you'll both laugh and joke and the urgency of his drinking will fade.

He'll invite you to his house for coffee but you will demurely decline as remarkably you still have some common sense left.

You'll plan to spend the next evening with some female friends in Cuban Heels just in case you're getting too carried away with all the attention. At the eleventh hour he will phone you and tell you that something life shattering has happened to him that day, but the phone just isn't the same and he would really like to talk to you face-to-face. You'll give in and put up very little resistance, after all you can have a girls' night another time. This will be the beginning of your demise, but you won't realise it.

He will come round to your house and suggest you go out for a drink at the Elbow Rooms. His mood will have altered slightly from the phone conversation and he will seem almost morose. You will ask him how he got on that day which was the purpose of his visit, but he will have lost interest. He will suggest you both play pool and while you rub chalk on your cue he will down a couple of pints of lager. The look on his face will change and he will appear almost mean. He will not be so attentive to your needs, but instead will pass you his empty glass when he's finished. At this stage you should say goodbye and at least wait three days till you see him again and have analysed his moodiness.

At this point Debra will ask you why you are seeing him every day and not making him wait. Whatever you do, don't mention the fact that you've agreed to meet him the next day for lunch.

You will spend every evening at his house because it's more private than yours. But as you are allergic to the hamsters he keeps in a cage you will sleep with the window open, which will be cold. And you will have to be up and out by 8 am every day before his ex-wife brings their twins round. He will tell you the last thing he needs right now is some kind of confrontation.

In the evening you will potter about his flat as if you've known him all his life. You'll be impressed by his array of plants and that he grows his own herbs. Later you will discover that some of the plants are marijuana and that he dries what he grows before he smokes and he smokes six times a day.

Several days later when you are out for an evening drive to Temple Newsam he will be so stoned that he will leave the keys in the car and lock them inside while you both take a leisurely stroll in the grounds.

You will then feel the heat of his temper as he shouts and curses at you for rushing him and making him forget. All sorts of reasoning on your part will not reduce his rancour. He will not think that maybe after three beers and two large joints he may be partially responsible.

You will phone a friend to drive him home so he can pick up a spare set of keys. He will finally manage to get into his car and drive you home, but he will not thank you.

The next morning when he is frying the bacon he will mumble away to himself that he must remember and not let you get the better of him. Although you will have saved his backside the day before, the whole episode will be entirely your fault.

If you're sensible you will take time out and think about the kind of man you are getting involved with.

Although it's your birthday you tell him you don't want to see him and that you have no plans. You hope that other friends will remember and you will go out with them for a change. If you are very unlucky, they will forget and have nothing planned. You will lay in your bed depressed and not know how to get out of it. You will succumb to phoning him and suggest he comes over as you could really do with some company. Debra will pop in on her way home from work and be delighted that you have invited him over. There won't be much food in the house and so what you throw together won't be very tasty. You will wish you had gone to Morrisons and bought something halfway decent. You and Debra will set the table and she will ask you if you want to invite anyone else round to make more of a party. You will agree as you will have to concede that desperate measures are required.

He will turn up late in his Citroen, two-and-a-half hours after you phoned him in fact. He will have parked it at the gate but you will be waiting on eggshells for him to come inside.

At this point Debra will be excited for you and encourage you to go outside and see what's keeping him.

You will be relieved to see him and will say hello and ask him what he's doing. The mean look will be back on his face and he will slam the door, only to realise that yet again he has locked himself out. Again he will be angry and blame you for distracting him with your hellos. He will thump the side of his car in frustration and you will instinctively move out of the firing-line.

You will go into the kitchen and tell Debra that he is really angry and that you're not quite sure what to do. She will not have seen the meanness on his face and will think you are over-reacting. At this stage remember how mean he looked.

You will all sit out in the street of your back-to-back until he manages to sort himself out and you can relax. He will have bought you an expensive bottle of wine and a handmade card, which will warm your heart and make you glad you invited him. He will join the little party and after a few drinks he will soften and your other two friends will be laughing at his anecdotes. You will not enjoy the wine he brought you. It will taste bitter, but you will say that you do.

After this you will follow a pattern. Every time you try to gather some space he will cry and tell you he is so depressed and still bruised from his last relationship that you will cave in and offer your shoulder. Then when he has toughened up, the meanness will spread across his face and he will try to blame you for all his insecurities. If you're very strong you'll break for the border but if you are in anyway sentimental you will stay and try to cure him.

You'll become more and more run down until the day comes, when Debra goes away on holiday and he will come round one evening. He will be tired and worn out and will have been in heavy discussions with his ex-partner who wants to make another go of it. The meanness on his face, which appeared when he was talking about her, will now appear when he is talking to you.

He will now blame you for the wrong turn his life has taken and how little old you will be the reason he hasn't achieved, how many goals?

He'll let rip that you are why he hasn't been taking care of himself recently and going to the gym as often as he used to. He won't hold back when he tells you that under no circumstances are you going to wrap him round your little finger.

His ranting will sound so absurd that you will not know how to react. You will think he's joking but you will not believe it when he turns round all six foot of him and punches you in the face for smiling at him in what he describes as a strange way. Your face will sting but you will ignore the stinging and use all your wits to calm him down so that he doesn't hit you again.

At this point you will have no alternative but to leave. He will cry and say he is sorry but you will realise that it's too late for sorrys.

A year later when you've just about forgotten him, you will see him driving his Citroen up the York Road. You will wave at him without thinking but then you will see the mean look in his eye, his unkempt beard and large teeth and you will stop waving.

Fortunately he will not see you, but you will wonder who he is blaming now for losing his keys and smiling.

Submarium
Lee J Harrison

Throughout the summer of 2001, Sarah felt the coming of *The Deep* to almost biblical proportion, and wondered if it really could change her life. Its angular structure jutted out from the banks of the Humber and Hull like a shard of outer space, the tip of an iceberg from the future. The Deep was a gigantic angular thing of steel and glass, building itself over the months and erupting from the land where disused docks had long since dried up. The Deep was the world's only *submarium*. No one knew what that meant, but never mind; it had the deepest aquarium exhibits in all of Europe. It would house marine life from across the globe, from the cold and brackish estuaries of the North Sea to the reaches of the Pacific; old world cod and new world creatures and colours, sand tiger sharks, rays and anemone. It would form links with business, education and research, it would be a place for men in suits to come and see, and it would all be in 'ull.

Sarah spent weeks at home, pretending she didn't suspect that Dean had lost his job again, whilst he was out pretending he was at the job he'd lost again, and the funny thing was, she could hear it, the bubbles, the sound of the waves. She stared blankly around the house and drifted on a current towards the window, as if she might see aquaria out there. But there, as ever, was Woodcock Street.

There were some kids, seemingly ever present, interchangeable scruffs in tracksuits lingering at the end of the block where the corner house had been demolished. They cowled over their bottles of Hooch, taking dares to throw a bent bicycle frame out in front of passing cars. You could still make out the stairs in the wall of the last house standing, and see the kitchen tiles still in place on the outside. Beyond that, a crumbling wall slouched to reveal the blackened eyeholes of the most recent empty house to be set fire to.

The corner shop had just recently closed, having been abused, broken into and worn down to ruin. The council had the whole street earmarked for demolition but did nothing, left it standing. For the people who still lived here, in between the abandoned wrecking houses, the street sometimes felt as if it was on death row. The wind blew cold off the Humber, but somehow didn't seem as loud or as nasty as the wind that blew through the disembowelled houses.

Sarah had been to see The Deep throughout its construction, especially at night, when it was lit up and beautiful, reflected in symmetry by the inky river. It scared her. She knew instantly, as much as she'd ever known anything, that she wanted to be a part of it, but opportunity seemed somehow alien and threatening. The day the phrase 'a job at The Deep' found purchase in her mind had made her mad and joyful, afraid and resentful. And Dean was easily irritated and resentful of all talk of 'that' The Deep. He never said so explicitly, but Sarah could tell by the way he made sure to refer to it always as '*that*' The Deep; as if it wasn't real, as if it was something he didn't understand or acknowledge. *That* Deep. *That* Father Christmas shit. She knew that this was something she wanted, this impossible thing, to be a part of the educational, international, seven-seas-and-five-continents phenomena, never known before in these forgotten parts. And so Sarah had bucked up her ideas. She pulled out her old CV. She put herself on the mailing list and collected newspaper clippings and flyers. She went to a careers fair and spent nearly two hours talking to the staff there.

The Deep was frightening in another way. The visionaries claimed that this would put Hull on the map, would aid Hull's bid to be a top ten city. But when she thought about it, where had we been all these years? Hull was on the map as some place that *used to be*, used to be fishing and all that, fish trade, blah-blah-blah. But now, Sarah couldn't ever remember what there actually was in Hull before this Deep Millennial Age. Some vague, before-her-time mental image of fishing boats and the Town Docks Museum was all there was. After the bombs of 1941, nothing.

Ten years ago it had seemed we were going somewhere when the shops began to open, shops that you'd only previously been able to see in other towns, in London, Manchester, Leeds. But once we got our Princes Quay Shopping Centre and a Starbucks, it became obvious that shops do not make a mark on the map. If you woke up on a street outside Maccy-D's and Topshop, it could be Rotterdam or anywhere, Liverpool or 'ull.

So where have I been all these years? wondered Sarah.

She couldn't remember much about where she'd been either. There was the olden days, represented by Jason Vickers, who she saw even now, hanging about there with the kids, one eye on her house yet again. She saw him glance over, and turned away to occupy herself.

In the olden days she'd been a precocious sixteen year old with Jason and the other kids, playing Block or Kerbie down on Ena Street. Once they'd played spin the bottle, and Jason Vickers, being only ten at the time, had kissed Sarah in the level-three-with-tongues round.

That was about all she could remember before now.

She could tell that Jason had never forgotten that. He was a peripheral figure now, a worn version of the child's face she'd forgotten, waiting outside on a Thursday for Dean to come home, maybe to sell him an eighth. But Jason looked at her boldly now, with the eyes of a man rather than blushing boy. And she'd noticed him as well, looking lean, keen, far different from the glazed dope-eyes and pot-bellied stillness that Dean had taken on. It irritated her that Dean noticed nothing, just sold on to this rival whatever he hadn't already smoked. But there were always eyes waiting to notice around here. Always someone who knew, or who knew someone else who knew. A dirty big goldfish bowl.

Dean's mam Edna wandered from one house to the next on a knock-and-enter basis, arms folded, sucking on a fag and scrounging the next one, up early to sign on at the top of the week, then nothing better to do than tell the neighbours what she thought of the other neighbours, drink tinnies with the neighbours, fuck the neighbours, whatever it was that microcosmic week. Edna ventured as far as The Boulevard, even visiting Jason's mother, then back. Everyone knew everything. But the Woodcock Street everything had nothing to do with *that* Deep.

Sarah rummaged through the spilling VHS cassette cases, noticing with a sigh the increasing amount of anonymous videos cropping up around the house, MIKES TAPE. FIST 3. He couldn't even be bothered to hide them anymore.

She tidied them away dutifully, sighing again as she thought of the usual. Her sitting awake upstairs in bed waiting for him, whilst he watched porn, smoked dope and tossed himself off. It wasn't worth challenging him. Dean's default reaction seemed to be frustration and anger. She would smile though these days and think of those aquaria, wondering if they switched the lights off at night, and how exciting it was to have tropical eels and sharks in Hull, there in the dark on the banks of the Humber.

Dean had a forklift licence but no incentive to shift himself. Since they'd moved in together, she had harassed and harried him to work; written his CVs and pushed him out of bed in a morning, nagged him to pay bills. But since the announcement of The Deep, things had changed. She'd left him to it, beginning to resent having to guide him in life. She'd grown weary, and more than a little scared of his furious reaction to the slightest question or challenge. And it was as if he sensed it, this threat from the bottom of the sea, curling his lip at the mention of *that* Deep, using her information pack for a roach, using her application form to line the cat's litter tray, as if he daren't vocalize the truth about his objection himself. Dean had never seemed more scared and helpless.

Last Thursday, it had officially come out about Dean's job, when she'd caught him.

***

Britannia House was a dinosaur building, a soulless monument to the square and concrete city centre. When the Queen had come to visit, seeing fit to visit some old biddy on Bransholme, she'd be passing this road on her royal route, so they tore up the bushes that used to be outside here and replaced them with a monumental pillar, a big industrial funnel thing painted blue like something from the set of a children's TV programme. This pillar of presentation was accompanied by some globular fountains that sprayed bleached water all over the pavement and the road. They straddled Britannia corner like three lactating tits. But Britannia House still lurked like an ugly concrete skag token booth.

'What the fuck are they anyow?' Dean was saying to Jason Vickers, looking at the slimy tit-fountains.

Sarah had caught them on the way out. They'd been averting their eyes from the women behind the plexiglass so they could make a straight-faced claim, up to where the message...*ALL CRISIS LOANS AND SOCIAL FUNDING ENQUIRIES TO DESK 7*...buzzed along like a lifeline on a heart monitor. They also averted their eyes away from the doormen so they could light up. Their eyes were so averse after Britannia that they couldn't walk straight, much less notice Sarah. And so Dean, who was supposed to be at work, was caught red-handed with a wad of Incapacity Benefit claim forms. Vickers, feeling strangely guilty as well, was there claiming a crisis loan, he said, to go to his Grandma's funeral in Newcastle.

The stupid thing was that after the initial discovery, she was calm about it, as ever, trying in vain to diffuse Dean's paranoia and frustration. *It's okay Dean, I worked out that you'd lost your job. It's okay, we can sort it.* She could sigh, swallow her vitriol and do this for him. But Dean was volatile, Dean denied that he'd been lying about his job, resented the implication, and so spun a thousand new lies. 'Oh, I've just come to get some advice on sick leave, oh, I've been sacked but it was only last week and I'm sorting it out with them now.' Lies and more lies, and what was more, the blame turned back on her. *You silly fucking bitch, stop fuckin' naggin', I'll sort it, don't you dare call me a liar*, shouting, shouting louder and closer into her face.

So, apart from being too scared and embarrassed to be shouted at in the street like that, she'd been willing to play armistice for the good of the relationship and he'd stormed off with Vickers to the pub, all victimized by his nagging girlfriend.

All the while, Vickers had a right eyeful of her, unguardedly, from top to toe. But Jason looked into her eyes as well, as if he *wanted* to, as if he even knew what colour they were, as if the green reminded him of that spun bottle. But she'd gone home, playing happy, but found herself there again, pretending, daydreaming about the oceans, until the feeling came to start worrying about tea.

So she dared to call Dean later on his mobile, to ask about when he was coming home. She just had time to hear the crack of a pool cue and the clink of a pint glass, then him. When drunk, Dean was a thousand times worse, and he kicked off at the very sound of her voice, how dare she f-ing check up on him, shouting, smashing down his phone. Sarah worried, and thought again about maybe going to stay with her mother instead of waiting for him to slam through that door. But she couldn't; she'd done that before, and that made him worse, charging around to her mother's and banging on the windows, *come out y' silly fuckin' cow, come out or I'll kick the fuckin' door in*. So she waited with her bowels churning, all so she could pad around him, flinching until they went to bed, and then he'd roll over and do a shag in her, his way of apology, his way of affection, his way of saying *no fucking more*.

But no. Last Thursday he'd been with Vickers, and Vickers had been fired up with the thought of these *moshers* who'd been looking at him in the Burger King the night before. Shitty moshers, with their black hoodies and massive black jeans, chains, skateboards and *Nu-metal*. Vickers had been pissing on Prospect Street near the Burger King as they went past, these moshers, and they stepped away from his salty, steaming urine as it gushed over the pavement. Just a look of distaste, that's all it had been.

As Vickers scurried after Dean on their way from the Eagle Tavern, down the bottleneck alley between Coltman and Saner Street, they'd happened to see, and point out with incredulity, these same moshers in their black hoodies. Beany, who had been sealed up with fuming irritation since hanging up on Sarah and leaving the pub, walked straight into the biggest one. He told them he'd been rowing with his lass. They tried to sidestep, shaken by this full-grown man starting on them. He and Vickers stopped them passing, using their *British Bulldog* sidestepping skills from the golden olden days of Ena Street. Dean thought of Sarah pushing him in to work, wanting to know what he was doing, where he was going, where his money had gone, don't eat this, don't take that... He told the moshers what he was about. Sorry, mate. Can't hit a lass. And then he took it out on them.

***

She'd taken herself as stunned, maybe depressed later that night. She was just settling, relaxing a little, knowing he was in a cell for the night, when there was a knock at the door and she found Vickers there, slightly out of breath. Sarah had already received the call from Edna. 'Our Dean's been locked up for fightin' again,' she droned. 'They're keepin' 'im in ovvanight. 'E's in court tomorrer morning.' Then the old cow had added: ''E was frightend to ring you cos you've been upset with him. So I'm ringin' yer.' Sarah laughed. *He* was frightened?

She was a little wary of Jason at first.

The kettle and the light switched on, the curtains drawn, and he filled her in on the details. The moshers had put up a wretched fight and run on to a barbeque they were heading to. Beany had marched in, having lost it completely. He ended up trying to push the smaller mosher's face into the barbeque. Jason described it with a feral kind of relish that made Sarah feel weak – she could imagine the shock to this innocent little soiree as these two stormed in through the rickety gate. The hot crackle and pop as the poor kid vomited, the smell of steaming, sizzling BBQ bile in the charcoal. The stand had collapsed before Dean could push the kid's face down. 'Good job,' Jason said. 'That woulda been GBH.'

The police had found Dean on his way home. He'd had a go at them as well. Vickers had long since legged it.

''E's always 'ad that temper though, 'as Beany,' said Jason. 'I remember the fuckin' day he pushed the fuckin' 'istory teacher through the fuckin' winder.'

'He's *never* changed.' Sarah spoke so matter-of-factly, and looked away in a moment of shame, not feeling anything much except a sense of anxiety at not feeling much. The room seemed somehow darker with the electric light on. She didn't want to be alone.

'So what you doin' with a caveman like that then? I mean, 'e's a mate and all that, but...' Jason sipped his tea and watched her sidestep his question.

'So how long has social been paying for my house?'

Jason shrugged, feeling guilty again.

Sarah shook her head, feeling that even talking about Dean would suffocate her. She dreaded finding out. She dreaded having to tell her mother and she dreaded the business of hiding it from her mother. Sarah's mother already spent her days shuddering from wall to wall, rattling like a tub of Beta-blockers.

So she sat quietly whilst Jason talked. He told her that he argued with his mam, who was, he reckoned, tight, and nosey, and stupid, and who had started screwing some silly old bastard from across the road. Sarah had in fact, already heard this from Edna. Jason said that his sister was a silly cow who was going nowhere. Both of them, nowhere.

He'd awoken that morning to find Edna at the front gate, already loaded up with a six-pack of tinnies, moaning through the window to be let in instead of just knocking and waiting. He traipsed downstairs to the smoke-filled kitchen where they sat gabbing, still in his cap and pants, still sporting a semi on. Edna and his old lady were setting the estate to rights, slagging off some woman, the health visitor of this bloke across the road for giving snooty looks from behind the posh fucking hanging baskets. Edna moaned,

'Don't cross the Social, Karen. She can stop yer money y' know.'

Jason was bored already.

'Mam, make us some breakfast.'

'Make yer own fucking breakfast.'

'Lend us a fiver.'

He nagged until she shrieked, *F-off Jason.*

'Look, there's a letter 'ere fo-yer. Open it and shut up.'

So he sat looking at the letter and ate great overflowing mouthfuls of Coco Pops, ignoring the two women. His blotchy-legged sister had stormed in, demanding to know where her J-Lo poster had gone. Jason took offence, denying it was under his mattress, where he'd tucked it away ready for him to wank over the big famous tanned arse whenever he liked.

'Mebbe it's blown out the winder.'

She wouldn't lend him a fiver either.

The letter turned out to be from a solicitor representing his late father. Jason's dad Brian had been absent, having sailed fortnight-on, fortnight-off on oil rig standby boats all his working life. He was taken ill with cancer, and then it came out that he'd had a bit on the side up in Newcastle, a woman named Gloria who he'd been spending most of his shore leave with. Brian chose to go and live his last with Gloria.

'What's in it?' quizzed Edna. Jason could almost hear her withered neck extending out of its collar.

'Mind yer own fuckin' business.'

He didn't let on, but his dad had left him money, to be awarded on his twenty-first birthday, in a week's time.

'So I've got meself a bit of a nest-egg,' he finished.

Sarah woke up a little.

'When do you leave for Newcastle?'

'Y' what?'

'I thought you had a funeral…you said…'

Vickers laughed. 'Nah. I never knew me nan. Just couldn't wait 'til next fuckin' week…' He made a mock toke with his fingers, and gave a cheeky look before standing. 'Newcastle was the furthest place I could think of,' he shrugged.

Sarah sighed and smiled a dry smile, not really very amused. Jason removed his cap and stretched, making as if to leave. She could see his wiry abdomen.

'You look better without that shit hat Jase,' she said, standing up to meet him. He looked in to the bottle green once again, and threw his cap down without protest, feeling suddenly that he was *in there*. He kissed her softly, and she laughed to feel downstairs activity jabbing her in the leg almost instantly. He told her he'd had a hard on for her for eleven years, ever since round-three-with-tongues on Ena Street. She laughed. It was the most heartfelt and passionate thing she'd heard in years.

***

That had been last Thursday. She'd gone the next day to see Dean in court. It was all so blustery and run-of-the-mill that it didn't register. Indifferent lawyers milling through corridors talking down to and through people. Tab ends outside. Dean hardly even looked at her, as if the whole thing was her fault. Past offences taken into account. Remand in custody. Two weeks in custody and then full sentencing on March 17th at two o'clock, which the solicitor said would likely be lessened from assault to affray, and consist of fines, community service, slap on the wrist. Sarah came home and sat with her leaning plant, feeling absolutely nothing.

***

Since last Thursday Jason Vickers had found his life. He was there all the time like some sentinel, pretending to be one of the fourteen year-old shits under an ineffective curfew that had trashed the street. He'd redeemed his inheritance money, and been round in nice new clothes that made Sarah laugh. She didn't want to let him in, good though it had been. Yes, Jason Vickers was as far back as she could remember but she didn't want to go back there. That wouldn't put her on the map, now would it? He stared shamelessly at their house. He turned up in a souped-up Corsa. He turned up with wads of cash. He sent her tastelessly large bunches of flowers. And at the weekend he'd texted her incessantly, *come out with me, come out 2nite, can I come back 2 yors, are U in, what U doin*, until Sarah switched off her mobile, and left it off. Jason turned up drunk on her doorstep at three o'clock in the morning in a miserable state, saying he loved her, and they could have a future together, they could be away before Beany got out, he could put a deposit on a house somewhere miles away, elope somewhere, East Hull maybe, his cousin's on Longhill. But with all he'd bought, smoked, drunk, taken, Sarah doubted Jason Vickers could afford the deposit on a pool cue. He stood outside regardless, looking lost, as aimless as he was with money or without, still not wearing his cap in some vain demonstration of affection. But somehow, she felt calm with him standing there like a piece of street furnishing.

It now seemed like forever since last Thursday, and everything before seemed like a grey area, like Hull before The Deep. It wasn't shock, or depression that had stalled her. She was excited like never before.

After Jason drifted off last Friday she flaunted her secret literature. She spread out her cuttings and pamphlets, maps, postcards and flyers, displayed The Deep in all its promotional glory. She binned MIKES TAPE. She tidied the house, and packed all but the clothes she would need for the next week or so. She didn't think through exactly why. She read the electricity and gas meters, and pulled out all the job descriptions for The Deep. Early Saturday morning, just because she could, she went to look at it: The Deep. From up the river, near the tidal barrier, it reflected, caught clouds and shades of blue like a net full of sky. From the opposite bank of the River Hull, it looked like a shark's head rising from the water.

Sarah saw Edna on the way back. This next rising shark was subtle. Edna took a puff on her cigarette, and gave a baleful sideways look towards her, nothing more. No 'hello', no 'why aren't you answering the phone?', no 'what about my Dean?', just a *look*. One for Sarah, and one demonstrative glance, towards Jason, who was still propped against the end house. As she exhaled, and traipsed off without looking back, she didn't even have to look back at Jason trotting across to her like a puppy dog. She'd seen enough to guess at enough scandal to fill her jobless, house-hopping, shit-stirring life for the next five years.

Sarah felt the panic for the first time. She couldn't even string words together for Jason, and got rid of him rudely. Then she fell over it - a letter stamped with the bubbling Deep logo – an invitation to interview. It was only a reception and admin job, but Sarah did not care. It was the impossible. She felt a sense of exultant joy. Then a diving, skull-cracking sense of sickness, as the date given was

Monday March 17th, 2.00 pm

That night, against her better wishes, Sarah was tempted to ring Jason. She writhed and tormented herself with memories of their night together. She tried to sleep and rest, and think of those soothing, Deep waves. But she dreamed of drowning now, and later in the night she awoke in a breathless panic. She twitched her curtain and looked out onto the orange street corner spotlight Jason had inhabited recently, her suitor, who was always there, serenading her silently amongst glittering shards of showbiz glass.

But he was gone.

***

March 17th. The day ended, clear and simple, at dinnertime when Sarah switched her phone on for the first time in nearly two weeks. It began to bleep, and sing and vibrate and pull at her almost immediately. Voicemails. Text messages, bombardments in no particular order.

WERE R U?

Dean's text messages always came in abrupt, shouting capitals.

ITS OK GOT REMAND + COMUNATY SERVICE

Though dressed up to the nines, Sarah felt like a giant bowel. She'd been ignoring the phone every night between six and eight. But he'd remembered her mobile, and the sheer volume of voice messages, one for every day he'd been inside, overwhelmed her. In preparation for her interview, Sarah listened to his torrent of abuse. He'd heard about Jason, yet his text about the court hearing wasn't hostile, and it was the not knowing what to expect that made her have to get off the bus and vomit.

Twenty minutes into what should have been her interview, Sarah leaned on the railing opposite The Deep, with irrelevant interview revision still swirling in her head. It was a dark, grey day. The mobile began again, always the same pattern. It rang. It went to answer phone. Then a text.

BITCH I NO ABOUT U + VICKERS SLUT SLAG

She'd stopped reading them. It still rang and it texted and

buzzed. The wind howled as if in irritation. The Deep sat calmly, with engine noises issuing from the construction going on behind it and under the wind, as if it promised to pull away at any moment, last chance boarding.

WERE THE FUCK R U? YOUR DEAD

The Deep's knife edge profile jabbed at the sky. Sarah stood looking out over the Humber, trying desperately to see what it was pointing at.

***

She walked home. On the short terrace where the burnt-out house slumped, she waited in a final moment of doubt and panic. Her eyes fixed on a dead bird in the middle of the fireman-trampled lawn. It was long dead, and the delicate bones of the broken wings made it look like a harp. It played anaesthetic sounds in her head as she stepped out in view of the house and walked across the crunching glass, her intestines squirming like a hooked worm. She could already feel fingers in her throat.

But as she approached, she heard the worst sound. Dean was slumped in the hallway sobbing. He was thin and grey, wracked by moans and shuddering gasps coming from lungs that would like to give in. She found him there, sitting amongst crumpled tab ends that he'd part-smoked before stubbing them out on his skin. She could see fragments of broken house overflowing into the hallway. He came crawling towards her like some vile and desperate Gollum, barely intelligible at first in words, but full of pitiful begging, and even more pitiful promises, *I promise to sort myself out, I promise to look after you, I'll treat you right, I won't smoke no more, please don't leave me for him I can't cope without you, I'll kill myself I will I'm so sorry…*

He stank of drink. As she went over to him, feeling more like a

117

front line medic than a consoling lover, she saw her houseplant shattered and smashed across the floor, soil scattered across the table and the skirting boards, broken leaves, shards of plates, and a spider-web crack in the TV.

An invasive gust of wind followed her in. It whipped her hair around her face, hinted at some urgency, a time to run. But Sarah stood through it all like a ship's captain going down.

The wind came one last time, billowed through their hallway and slammed the door shut.

If There is No Justice

Tom Palmer

'My client would like, first of all, to apologise unreservedly to the court for missing his hearing of the 16th of April...'

Rob looks round Court One of Leeds Magistrates. At a solicitor's mouth working. At men in pinstripe suits, flicking through piles of paper. At the three magistrates, *Mon Dieu Et Mon Droit* on the wall behind them. He is nervous. He hasn't been in this court before and is studying the hard varnished wood, the blue-veined mock marble pillars, the glass cage for prisoners.

'However...'

Rob sighs, corrupting the solicitor's pause. The usher eyes him.

'However, your worships, Mr Denholme was incapable of attending court on the said date.'

The middle magistrate cocks his head to one side. Rob looks at the boy in the dock. Thin. Ugly. Short. Pale skin. Spots. Rob shuffles in his seat: he has a good feeling about this case.

'On the day of his court appearance Mr Denholme was physically debilitated by a recurring case of curvature of the spine from which he has suffered for several years, and for which I have medical evidence provided by both Mr Denholme's GP and St James' Hospital, Leeds.'

The magistrate nods.

'As a result of his difficulties, my client was unable to attend court to face the charges of shoplifting, which, as you will see, your worships, he committed solely to fund his addiction to heroin, for which he is now receiving treatment. To compound his back pain,

121

his parents were away, and, as his situation became worse, Mr Denholme was unable to make it downstairs to where the telephone is situated, and was thus unable to call the court, your worships.'

A junkie, thinks Rob. A fucking junkie.

'For how many days were you so marooned, Mr Denholme?' The middle magistrate.

The solicitor answers: 'Three days your worship. Mr Denholme was only able to make it to the bathroom, to use the lavatory and to drink water from the upstairs sink. I would like to repeat that Mr Denholme respects the will of the court, but would argue that he was unable to comply with its rules. He would like – again – to apologise. And I would request that he is allowed bail before the date of his full hearing.'

The magistrate thanks the solicitor and begins talking to his two colleagues.

Rob smiles. He knows that this boy in the dock could be the one. He has sat through two previous cases – a drug dealer kept on remand and a burglar jailed for three months – neither of them any good. If they let this one off, Rob thinks, I'm in business. He is almost grateful for the weasel words of the solicitor. And he is pleased that the boy is a junkie. He hates junkies. They disgust him. They are the lowest of the low.

The solicitor's paperwork is handed to the magistrates. They consult again.

'The court agrees to bail. Mr Denholme will be released and should return to court on…'

Rob blanks the rest, exploding with adrenaline. But he must wait for the right moment. Would the man be released in the court or taken downstairs? He looks at the boy and sees the trace of a triumphant smile. The boy is asked to stand, which he does with a grimace. But he's feigning. He's not disabled. He is a wimp, yes. A boy. But not a cripple.

Rob leaves the court as the boy falls into discussion with his solicitor. He will wait for him outside.

Three hours earlier Rob is on Briggate.

The street is a corridor of cold shadow, the sun too low to reach over its buildings at seven in the morning. Rob stands in front of Harvey Nichols, looking again for tyre tracks on the road surface. But there is nothing. He finds the spot where he thinks Adele must have died. He imagines a white van coming out of Harvey Nichols' shattered glass, turning to go left down Briggate, then hitting her.

Briggate is busier than he would like it to be. He should have come earlier. One morning he came for dawn. Five a.m. He can't locate Adele surrounded by all these people. He wishes he could have one conversation with her. Just one. So that he could explain. But she is dead.

Adele was Rob's girlfriend. They met when she was temping and he was in the stationery room at Wetherall's, where he still works. They lived together in Harehills. Then they finished. Then she was killed by a van escaping a ram-raid with over two hundred brightly coloured handbags and a rack of sunglasses. It is her funeral tomorrow.

Rob looks down Briggate, the shop fronts alternating brick, glass, brick, glass, brick, glass. He is still in cold shadow, but at the intersections of the Headrow and Kirkgate shafts of sunlight illuminate the people walking to work clutching paper cups.

A group of men erect fencing in front of Harvey Nichols. Huge pieces of metal clanking as the men grip them together. Hoardings inform shoppers that they must not stop shopping, that everywhere is *Open For Business As Usual.* Rob remembers shopping with Adele. Sometimes just with her. Sometimes with her sister, Karen too. Round and round boutiques and department stores, nodding approval, but sometimes shaking his head to show he really liked the ones he said he liked. Aware of Adele and Karen. Their figures. Their clothes. Their hair. Aware that he was a man shopping with two good-looking women, other men looking at him. But half the shops today – ENVY, ASPECTO, KOOKAI – are new. Names that mean nothing to him. He has never been in them and now he never will. Their windows are explosions of colour. Purples. Pinks. Oranges. And Rob wishes they had ram-raided one of these, then Adele might have just stood and watched them fill the back of their van with neatly folded piles of t-shirts and racks of see-through skirts. Even though he hadn't seen Adele for months, he misses her more acutely now she is dead.

Tomorrow he will come earlier, he decides. He will arrive before it is light. No workmen. No early office workers. No to-go coffee drinkers. None of these men around him, wearing STREET CLEANSING SERVICES on their backs, picking scraps of rubbish off the pavement. Rob thinks they should concentrate on the drunks and junkies and ram-raiding scum before they worry about last night's newspapers and burgers. So far the police had done nothing about Adele. They haven't even traced the van. They knew nothing. But Rob is not surprised. He has seen the crime pages of the *Yorkshire Evening Post*. He has seen shoplifters chased by overweight security guards, seen cars driving in bus-only lanes, seen suitcases filled with stolen perfumes snapped shut as the police come round the corner. Leeds is filled with crime and the police do nothing. This is the truth. And if they do catch people, he thinks, they don't get punished. They get helped. They get rehabilitation. They get treatment for their drug addiction. They get poets-in-residence and visits by Premiership footballers. Then they are released, maybe a tag around their ankle, back onto the streets, onto their filthy drugs, into the crimes committed to pay for drugs.

But what could you do? Write to the *Yorkshire Evening Post*? Become a policeman? Do something about it yourself?

When he was younger, skipping classes at Park Lane College, Rob and his mates used to go drinking all day. When the pubs shut in the afternoon they would go to the Magistrates Courts to see people tried, waiting again for opening time. When the courts were in the Town Hall. Back then, he used to be on the side of the lads dragged up one after the other. Shoplifters. Football hooligans. Breachers of the peace. He used to be pleased when they were let off. They'd beaten the system. But not any more.

And standing on Briggate at seven-fifty in the morning, Adele dead, he realises he *could* do something about it himself.

Rob waits outside the court for the boy with the phantom curvature of the spine. The sun is beating hard on every street now. It's hot. Leeds smells like a foreign city. The Town Hall looks magnificent against the deep blue of the sky. In and out of the court's rotating door go young men and women with files and documents and expensive haircuts. The smell of their hair products competes with exhaust fumes. Rob sits at the foot of a staircase and wonders who designed this place, all marble pillars, soft lighting, six-foot waxy green plants, shining stone floors. He remembers the old Magistrates Court: leather seats with the stuffing coming out, old clocks that didn't work, faded carpets. The new place disgusts him.

The boy looks even smaller outside the court. Thin. Weak. Stupid. Rob remembers his expression when he was granted bail. His complacency. The look of impotence on the faces of the magistrates.

The boy walks towards the city centre. Alone.

Rob follows, thinking, has he seen me? Does he know what he is in for? And Rob wonders what he *is* in for. He has no plan. Just to follow. Find the chance to get back at one petty criminal junkie.

Up the Headrow, the road rises as he follows the boy past the Town Hall and Central Library. This part of Leeds is calm. No frenzy. No shops. He wonders if he should stop to think, maybe conjure Adele up here, away from the shoppers. But he can see the boy ahead of him affecting a slow pace, a swagger. He remembers the charges set against this boy: shoplifting, missing a court appearance. And he follows. Cars speed along the three carriageways into the city centre. Rob counts four with England flags flapping. There are flags in shop windows too. In bakeries, cafés and photocopying shops. Everywhere, huge displays using football to sell books, clothes, beer, CDs, computer games, bank accounts, stationery, electrical goods. Anything people have to sell or may be willing to buy.

Up past the great big shopping centre on the right. The bus lanes. Shoppers carrying fancy bags with fancy names – KAREN MILLEN, GAP, ZARA. Everyone in the way. A woman with a stick, stopping to stand unsteadily when people come near her. Two old men, brothers, their faces the same, wearing jumpers and jackets even in this heat. Girls with dyed blonde hair everywhere. An overweight child eating a pasty. A priest with a rucksack.

The boy takes a right down Lands Lane. Into the heart of town. Rob is twenty yards behind when his target cranes his neck and looks him right in the eyes.

He knows, Rob thinks.

The boy picks up his pace and weaves across the road. He's going to make a sudden run for it. Rob can feel adrenalin building in his muscles: he is ready.

Walking quickly down the slope, Rob can feel his feet hitting the street. He thinks of his weak footballer's knee. That he did it the same weekend as Gazza. Years ago. He glances left down a side street to see Briggate, where he'd been this morning. He thinks of Adele. He is doing this for Adele. One correction in a city of a million mistakes. The boy goes towards WHSmith. Can Rob do anything in there? Can he follow him into a shop? Beat him up in a shop?

Then a sudden move, the boy leaping over a row of benches down an alley. Rob is fooled, having to run round the benches. The boy is half-way down the alley, a dozen small plastic England flags fluttering in the half-light, half-shadow. And Rob is running. Running hard and fast. He sees drainpipes, bars on windows, a neat row of skip bins. Sees the boy's feet hitting the pavement ahead of him. Hears his footfall. Sees him disturb a drinker who spills a pint, calling after the boy. Then letting Rob pass without a word. They know, Rob thinks. They know I am Good chasing Bad. He feels his heart in his chest. Pain. Pain he likes. Like a shot of espresso. He is gaining on the boy, who has stumbled and is limping. A smear on the floor where he slipped.

Then left onto Briggate, from the shadow of the alley into the hot sun. Shoppers stopping to watch. Across the front of Monsoon, its riot of colours, summer dresses and parasols. The boy takes a left again, disappearing into a wall. Another alley. Cluttered with a dozen more skip bins. Rat poison boxes. The smell of baked bread. The sound of air conditioning units. Rob is gaining. The boy looks round. Then again. Ten feet. Fire exits. Six feet. Smashed plaster walls. Three feet. Breeze blocks. Red bricks. The boy is up against a skip bin. The sun on him like a spotlight. Rob pushes him back. He falls. Rob is kicking him. The sounds muffled by the air conditioning hum, the indifferent mutter from the street. The boy is down, staring back at Rob.

But Rob can do no more than kick a few times. He won't hurt him. He has done enough. Scared him. Corrected him. He kicks him a last time. But the boy has turned away, squinting into the sun. Waiting for me to go, Rob thinks. And he is aware of the sun raging above them, feels sweat running down his back, inside his jeans, on his neck. He can smell piss, hot in the sun. And his fear of rats crawling from the shadows sets him off. He walks quickly. Out into the street, among the shoppers. Briggate at midday in June. Trying to walk at a normal pace now. Trying to look normal. Trying to feel normal. His whole body writhing.

Rob waits for her outside her workplace. A tall black glass and red brick building with turrets. There was a nightclub called Madisons here before, he remembers. The shapes of men in suits stare down on the city from tinted windows. Rob doesn't know if it's a solicitor's or a bank or what. But he knows she works here, has her lunch at one, comes out alone and goes for a coffee. He has watched her – only watched her – day after day since Adele died.

'Karen?'

She looks at him. A girl slightly shorter than Adele. Thinner. Younger. Dark hair. Cut like the solicitors have it cut, he thinks. *Styled*, not cut. And seeing her up close again, her eyes, her mouth, the curl of hair against her face, shocks him. He feels tiny cramps through his body. A nausea. His heart pumping.

'Rob?'

'I thought I'd take you for lunch,' he says, immediately intimidated. Did he ever take anyone for lunch?

Karen half-smiles, thinking the same.

'You look terrible,' she says. She had prepared for this moment, intending to tell him to leave her alone, that she never wants to see him again. But she is moved by his ruffled appearance. She worries that he has been sleeping rough. And she remembers that not too long ago she loved him. Enough to risk everything.

'A coffee?' Rob says.

'I need something to eat,' she says.

Rob is desperate and points to *Est Est Est*, a restaurant across the street.

'There,' he says.

'There?'

'Yes. Lunch. All you can eat.'

Approaching *Est Est Est*, Rob feels anxious. Karen has said nothing. He is looking at the sheet glass windows that reveal a dozen tables of eaters, all white shirts and ties, looking out at the people walking by. One in three on a mobile phone. White table cloths. Cutlery. Crockery. Glasses for wine. Glasses for beer. Single flowers in narrow-necked vases. He is intimidated. He can smell Chinese food. Buses pull into a terminus to the right. Rob and Karen climb the steps, still nothing said. They are led to a table.

The conversation flounders: the sunny day, the football, her job. The drinks arrive. And Rob feels desperate.

'I want to start seeing you again,' he says.

'What?'

'Seeing you.'

'For God's sake, Rob,' she says. 'For God's sake.'

Rob sees a group of three men in pinstripe suits looking over. He thinks he recognises one from the courts. Full of self-importance in this restaurant for solicitors. Defending filthy junkies an hour ago in the Magistrates Courts, then coming here to eat on expenses.

'Everything okay, Karen?' one says. Dark hair, waxed, swept back over his head.

'Thanks Marco. Yes.'

Rob feels a huge desire to walk over to Marco's table and to turn it over, punching all three men before they can stop him. Marco! What sort of a fucking name is that? Rob is raging. He hates the tide of young men – solicitors – who have suddenly appeared in Leeds. Living in their lofts overlooking the station, flash cars in the garages underneath, taking all the city's money, all the city's women. Their steel and blonde wood bars displacing the old pubs: The Precinct, The Whip, The Jubilee. Pale and ugly men sat at fancy tables with extraordinary women.

'Rob. We will never have anything to do with each other again. Once…After tomorrow.'

The funeral.

'We were good,' Rob says, after hesitating.

'We were,' she says. 'When you were living with my sister.' Her voice is a whisper, but it makes him flinch.

'We…'

'No we. No *we*,' Karen hisses. '*We* killed Adele. Do you ever stop to think about that?'

'What are you talking about?'

'Think about it.'

'Neither of us…'

'Neither of us what? Were in Leeds that day? Is that what you were going to say? But she came in and saw us, Rob. In her bed.'

Rob feels sick. The memory always makes him feel sick.

Karen leans back, her eyes closed. Rob looks at her cleavage. He imagines Marco's hand slipping down the front of her top. He looks at Marco. Marco is still staring. Rob feels his legs go tense. He'd have Marco. Like the little worm he picked up at the court. He'd have Marco and every fucker he saw who he didn't like the look of. He stands to go over to the three men.

Then he hears Karen say heroin.

'What?'

'Adele was on heroin.'

Rob laughs.

'What sort of a relationship did you two have?' Karen says.

'What?'

'She never told you any of this, did she?'

'About what?'

'Rob. Before you came along she was doing heroin with Jack. You remember Jack, don't you? Me and Dad got her off it. Then after you and me did what we did she went straight back to him. Straight onto the heroin.'

'Come on!' Rob says, hearing his own voice like it isn't his. 'Why are you doing this?'

'She was a junkie, Rob.'

'No,' he says. The word disgusts him.

'Why do you think she didn't get out of the way of that van like the rest of them that day? Why do you think she just stood there like a…a zombie…and…'

Karen is crying now. Rob goes to comfort her, his hand across the table.

'Fuck off,' she says.

The restaurant is silent. Marco is standing over them.

'Did you hear what she said?' Marco says.

Forty to fifty people are staring. All in their fine suits and fancy ties. Cappuccino crockery and wine glasses trembling in anticipation. Karen is refusing to look at him, her eyes fixed on the tablecloth.

He walks across the city, stumbling towards people who know to move out of the way. Kids' shrieks fill his head. He sees turbans, briefcases, breasts, cigarettes going into mouths, cans of Coke, pigeons. Crossing Albion Street, heading towards Vicar Lane, he is caught in a cross-tide of shoppers and struggles to navigate through the two streams. He crashes into people, sees England shirts, patterns of gum mapped out on paving stones. Market researchers. Pushchair pushers. Big Issue sellers. And his head is filled with a montage of mobile phone conversations, each blending into the next.

On Vicar Lane, seeing the Parish Church down the hill, he is nearly knocked over by a bus, forgetting again its two-way traffic. Then across The Headrow and into The Hellenic Café. Where his mother used to take him when he had to go to the market with her on Saturdays. A cake and a can of pop, he was allowed. Rod Stewart playing on the radio. A smile from the woman who serves him his coffee. She calls him Love. He looks at the salt and pepper and vinegar pots on each table. The coat rack in the corner. Listens to the woman behind the bar addressing customers by their names. And he is thinking of Karen. What the fuck was she talking about? That they were to blame? He doesn't accept it for a minute. He wishes he'd turned Marco's table over. He knows they are shagging. She was always a slag. She fucked her sister's boyfriend, didn't she? Only a slag would do that. He wishes he'd kicked the shit out of Marco, right there in front of the massed clientele of *Est Est* fucking *Est*. He wishes he'd done a better job on the little shithead from the court too.

And he knows what he has to do next. So he doesn't have to listen to the voices in his head, the echoes of what Karen said.

He has to act.

He spots a wiry lad. Smaller than the last. Fed on junk food and heroin since he was a kid. He'd do.

The lad turns left out of the courts. Up Park Street. Alone. A quick pace. But Rob is onto him. Past the tall gates at the side of the courts, making him look even smaller. The featureless walls of the Crown Court opposite. A fortress. Three white vans waiting to take the convicted away. This one should be in there, Rob thinks. But, if the courts can't deal with him, he will. It will be his public service.

St George's Church to the left, the lad goes right. Rob stays on the other side of the road, tracking. The lad hasn't looked back, moving fast, towards the Merrion Centre. Rob realises he hasn't been there in years. He follows the lad along Great George Street. A thief? A junkie? A ram-raid driver? What does it matter? He's scum and he's next. Number two of hundreds of victims Rob will have. And this time he'll give him a proper beating. He'll be a one-man vigilante force. He'll start a trend. An alternative to the police and the courts. He'll become known. A deterrent. But the lad has disappeared. Somewhere around the back of the Town Hall. Rob is running. Is tripped. Is in a doorway. Him and the boy. The boy punching. Three to the head. Hard punches Rob can hear, but can't feel, not on his face, only across his back. Shouting words Rob can't make out. Three or four more blows, feeling like an iron bar across his back. And it's all so quiet and so bright.

Then the boy is gone and Rob is alone. He can hear quick footsteps. He looks up at The Victoria Hotel across the road. He has been drinking there dozens of times. He sits on the steps, feeling the contours of his face for wounds, feeling exhausted, tearful. Two people go by, seeing him, pretending they haven't. The next turns to help, but Rob looks down. He doesn't want help. He has worked out what Karen meant.

Between Hope and Paradise

Penny Feeny

5.30pm

Crossing Concert Square, Adam was already on guard. At this hour the mass of chairs and tables stood waiting for custom; there was no cover. But the boy had a habit of appearing from nowhere, as if he could grow out of a lamp-post or slither up from a manhole. He had a room in a hostel, but Adam suspected he more often slept in doorways so that he could always be alert, like a doctor on call. He turned the corner, the entrance to the bar only a few paces ahead. As he reached it, a dark shape slipped from the stone portico. 'See, I am ready,' it said.

The boy was a problem Adam hadn't yet solved. It was uncanny the way he knew all his shifts and the way he ignored all attempts at ejection. He flitted from table to table like a moth, collecting glasses, emptying ashtrays, mopping up spillages and Adam – supposedly in charge – didn't have the first idea how to stop him. The floor staff assumed he was on the payroll, the security staff had decided to let him get on with it. The lad was quick, obliging, no trouble. He had a way of ingratiating himself so that the others treated him like some kind of mascot: sharing out tips, making sure he was regularly fed in the kitchens. Adam was out-manoeuvred.

'It's early yet,' he said. 'There'll be nothing for you to do.'

Mahmoud had eyes as dark as treacle and the faint shadow of a beard along his jaw, a slight sinewy body, a feline grace. He claimed to be seventeen but looked older. He caressed Adam's arm with joyful familiarity and Adam flinched.

'I will help in kitchen. Is always need for cleaning.'

The broad staircase led to the series of cellar rooms that had been transformed by ingenious lighting, seating and ventilation into the Yellow Lounge. They walked down it together, but Adam pretended he was alone.

6.00pm

From the window Stella could see the river and the twin towers of the Liver building. That is, if she stood on the ledge which had once been a platform for bearing goods up and down the face of the old warehouse. Now, the addition of railings had transformed it into a balcony. Turning away from the view, back into a room so empty it echoed, she picked up her small suitcase. She took out her sponge bag and a towel and carried them into the bathroom. The shower was hot and fierce, a warm cloak of steam pierced by dazzling halogen lights. But when she stepped out of the cubicle to dry herself she shivered at the thought that she was the only person in the building. Who in their right mind would move into a vast brick carcass where no-one could hear you scream?

The flats were being fitted out and sold off by degrees. Only you weren't supposed to call them flats. She kept forgetting that. Apartments, lofts, penthouses – all had a better ring. She had been lent hers by a contact of Nick's. A guilt offering, she thought of it. She hadn't let him drive her here; she hadn't brought more than essentials from home. In the morning she'd see how the light fell, she'd go to Jackson's in Slater Street for supplies: for soft sable brushes and the consoling colours, vermilion, ochre, sienna, of oil paints. 'I don't see how this solves anything,' Nick had said.

She dropped the damp towel on the bathroom floor and wandered naked through the apartment. Everything in it was angular: the bed frame, the easy chairs, the coffee table; even the taps, the telephone, and the cupboard handles. In the mirror, her body, too, had lost its curves, become spare and lean. With hesitant fingers she traced a line from throat to thigh. Her flesh was cold and unresponsive; the tenderness of touch a distant memory. Quickly she dressed and tossed the suitcase into a closet that could have accommodated the stock of a small boutique. She left the long windows open: she had nothing to lose. Then she walked down the four flights of stairs and let herself out into the street.

7.00pm

The early evening lull. Adam enjoyed that. There were fewer offices at this end of town, so there was never such a crush of suits as when he'd worked in Victoria Street. He preferred people to dribble in by degrees, giving him plenty of time to assess them. He liked to stand at the corner of the bar watching the legs as they descended, liked trying to guess how the rest of the body might look.

This time he could tell, from the tap of heel and toe, before the legs even came into view, that his customer was a woman, on her own. Something in the way she sauntered towards him, the way she leant on her elbow, planting her chin on her hand, something in her breathy slightly petulant voice, stirred recognition. Not the face. Not the ripe-plum mouth. Not the hair, which had been through a myriad of styles and palettes. She fixed her eyes on his.

'Large vodka and tonic please.'

'Ice and lemon?'

'Thanks, Adam.'

Keeping his grip steady on the tongs, he dropped several ice cubes into a glass. 'Stella?'

'You haven't changed.'

'Much…' The sharp satisfying crack of the ice as the vodka was added. A splash of tonic: she wouldn't want it too diluted. He added an olive on a cocktail stick and a straw. 'How long's it been? Ten years at least?'

She removed the straw and took a long drink. 'I bumped into Phil the other day, remember? What did we call him, The Fixer? Anyway, he told me he'd heard you were back in Liverpool, working here. Nice to get the news third-hand.'

Adam shrugged. That was the way it was really. When he'd gone down south he'd said goodbye to old friends, been swallowed up by the maw that was London and hadn't expected to return.

'Hey, over here.' A large American was waving a large note. Adam was proud of his ability to anticipate custom and annoyed at the interruption. He moved away from Stella to serve the man and was about to call one of the girls over to help him behind the bar when she appeared miraculously, smoothing the front of her apron. 'Mahmoud said you wanted me.'

Adam, the manager, wanted to kick Mahmoud, the prescient unpaid skivvy, in the teeth. Instead he went back to Stella. She'd nearly finished her drink and there was a bright cocktail-hour fervour about her he distrusted. He'd put more tonic in the next one. 'Are you meeting somebody?' he asked.

'You don't believe I'd call in just to see you?' She twirled a set of keys on her middle finger. 'Actually, I'm celebrating.'

'Celebrating?'

'Independence Day.'

'Sorry love, you've lost me.'

'I've left him, Adam.'

'Who?'

'Nick, of course. You came to the wedding, remember?' She spun the keys again. 'I'm starting over.'

As a barman, Adam was used to outpourings of the recently

separated, though generally later at night than this. He made a non-committal grunt.

'I had this crazy plan,' she said. 'I thought maybe I could come back into town, rent my old studio and start painting again. Only I couldn't find it. I thought I was going crazy until I picked up one of these.' She fished a glossy brochure from her handbag. 'Don't you just hate the way all this sales-speak has divvied up the city into Quarters – as if we lived in fucking Paris. Who are they trying to fool? Now listen.' She was halfway through her list of security devices, polished granite surfaces, brushed steel appliances and breath-taking vistas when Mahmoud appeared with a long order for drinks.

'You are *not* supposed to take the orders,' said Adam.

'I sorry. They ask me.' A group of young men, jackets off, collars loosened, ties in their pockets, were calling for beers.

'Well, keep your distance next time.' Shit, he thought, as he handed Mahmoud the tray of drinks: open less than two hours and he was already losing control.

Stella was ripping the leaflet into tiny shreds and setting fire to it in the ashtray. 'I see some things don't change.'

'Meaning?'

'He's got a cute arse.'

'Fuck it! I can't get rid of him. He's hounding me.'

'Aren't you pleased that he fancies you?'

'I think he's trouble. I can't employ him: he's an illegal immigrant. God knows how he got into the country in the first place.'

'With the help of a jar of Vaseline, I expect.'

Adam raised his eyebrows. There was no rule that said you had to humour close friends you hadn't seen for more than a decade. What had got into her?

'Sorry, do I sound bitter?'

'Yes.'

For an instant the pain in her eyes scoured him until he felt the rawness himself. He was glad when a gaggle of girls who worked in the trendier shops of Bold Street – tattoos like badges on their arms, crystal studs flashing in their navels – clustered at the bar, changing their order every twenty seconds. As Adam exchanged Bacardi Breezers for Wkds and vice versa, Stella slipped off her bar stool and took her drink to the deep dim corner of one of the leather sofas.

7.30pm

Did money smell? Stella wondered as she watched clean notes being pulled out of wallets, bright rectangles of plastic tossed onto saucers. Or was it completely odourless, tasteless, silent as still water? Perhaps that was its power: the power to sanitise. Certainly poverty smelled. Her old studio, at the back of Parr Street, had been cold and dirty with a handsome variety of fungus growing on the walls. No hot water – but a huge cast-iron bath, in which she had tie-dyed and marbled the silk scarves everybody said were so exquisite but nobody could afford to buy.

She and Adam had met at the College of Art and become inseparable, drinking in Ye Cracke or the bar of the Academy, blazing with ambition and high hopes. He was supposed to be working on an enormous installation (if it was too big for the Bluecoat, maybe the Tate would take it) but he kept running out of cash for materials. And he was far too easily distracted. Life comes before Art, was his excuse every time he wanted a drink or a fuck.

Stella could still conjure the smell of poverty: mould and bad drainage and harsh cheap bleach. The sound of it was the wind wheezing through an ill-fitting windowpane and the scurry of rats.

There were a few derelict places the developers hadn't got around to yet, with grass growing in the gaps in the slates and a trickle of slime down the side of a wall. Soon enough they, too, would become lofty sterile spaces, gleaming with invisible money. But there'd always be a rank pocket somewhere, she reckoned. She knew, better than anybody, there were some things the freshest money couldn't buy.

Watching Adam now, she could see that although his hair was still glossy and his profile keen, he had a jaded air. The bar was buzzing with animation, with raucous reckless youth, but he moved from task to task mechanically, as if on autopilot. She realised then how much she had wanted him to be as he had always been: her companion in fun and frolic. The same.

Her phone rang, startling her. She took it out of her bag, saw that her husband was calling, and switched it off.

9.30pm

When he wasn't directing staff or filling glasses, Adam had time to notice Stella's consumption of vodka. He snapped his fingers at Mahmoud. Mahmoud sailed across the floor like a bat with inbuilt radar, smartly avoiding collision with skittish posers and heavy-footed drunks.

'See that woman there,' said Adam, indicating Stella, whose head was lolling a little in the corner of her sofa. 'I want you to take her a sandwich. Tell the kitchen to come up with something quick and substantial. Steak and onion maybe.' Or was she vegetarian? Shit, he'd forgotten. 'No, better make that mozzarella and roasted peppers. And tell her I said she had to eat it.'

'Woman with black hair?'

'Yes.'

'And so sad face?'

143

Stella's features were strong, arresting, but now looked crumpled. Adam shrugged. 'Seems her marriage has broken up. Whose hasn't? I just happen to know how easily she passes out, so do as I say, will you?'

When he saw Mahmoud leaning over her with the plate of food, tapping her shoulder as if to rouse her from sleep, he picked up a bottle of mineral water and two glasses and joined her on the sofa. 'It's my break now,' he said. 'Thought I'd check you were okay.'

'I'm fine.'

'Fill me in then. How's the business?'

It had taken off at the beginning of the nineties, just before he went down to London. Stella had graduated from scarves to other accessories: belts, hats, gloves. There was a brief period when nearly every girl shopping in Church Street had been wearing or buying one of Stella's hats.

She was eating, he noted with relief. She brushed crumbs from her lips, obediently drank the water he handed her. 'Went bust, didn't I? It was bound to happen sooner or later. I mean, there comes a time you have to move on. You expand or you get taken over or you go to the wall. Well, I went to the wall.'

'Tough shit.'

'It's not tough; it's business. And I didn't want to be a businesswoman. I wanted to be an artist, remember? Like you. So how come you're running a bar?'

'Well, what do you think?'

'I don't know, Adam, that's why I'm asking.'

The sofa was comfortable, yielding but firm. The early-evening after-work crowd had moved on. A new tranche of customers was settling in for the night. The hum of their voices spiralled into the vaulted ceiling; the mood was relaxed. Adam spread his arms. 'This is where the money is. Plus it's a ready-made social life – yes, I'm one of those poor fuckers.'

'And?'

'And then, the theory goes, during a long free afternoon when the light's good and I'm feeling fresh as a daisy, I can be creative again. Or not, as the case may be. You keep promising yourself… but hell, who keeps promises? Look, can I get you a coffee or something?'

'No thanks. I'm on a mission to get wasted.'

'Just so long as you don't puke over my shoes.'

This was a reference to the time, years ago, when he'd been trying to get her back from the pub to the studio. He'd rashly spent far more than he could afford on a pair of Italian leather boots and she had vomited spectacularly into the gutter where he had been standing. 'Fuck, you bitch,' he'd shouted, leaping backwards into the path of a passing car. The driver, being sober – and a trainee solicitor – had been anxious to make sure they were all right. He got out of his car, tried to pick them both up and prop them against the wall like puppets. Stella collapsed and Adam cursed his bruises. In the end the three of them trailed up the galvanised metal staircase that led to Stella's studio. She filled a bowl with cold water and dipped her face into it; then, in a gesture of atonement, she polished the vomit off Adam's boots with one of her finest pieces of silk. The driver parked himself on an old horsehair chaise longue, fascinated by the room that looked like a theatrical set, draped with velvet and faux furs, and by Stella. He asked if he could see her again. And although she told Adam he wasn't her type: too stocky, too freckled, too *earnest*, she agreed on a date. Two years later she married him.

Her mouth twitched at the recollection.

'So,' said Adam. 'What's brought this on? What did the bastard do to you?' Ever vigilant, he noticed her handbag yawning open like an invitation. He leaned across and snapped it shut. 'Couldn't keep his flies buttoned or what?'

She shuddered. 'Not exactly.'

He couldn't understand why she was so cagey. In the past they'd egged each other on to more and more extreme confessions. But blowing your mind was different then. Like blowing a stranger you'd met in some sweaty club only ten minutes before. Before there were repercussions. He felt an urge to confide in her, to encourage her confidence in return. 'Did anyone tell you,' he asked, 'why I'd come back from London?'

She shook her head with some difficulty as if it were too heavy for comfort.

He swallowed some mineral water, tried to keep his tone measured and even. 'Well... it was because I lost someone there. Someone who...' He'd been going to explain about Ben: the quality of the relationship they'd had, the fact that he'd lived with HIV for years, the assumption that he could continue to manage the condition, the shock of his relapse. His own dithering and attempts to continue as if nothing had happened.

But Stella interrupted. 'For Godsake don't sound so twee. And please don't tell me he passed away.'

Adam gaped, astonished.

'Tell me he died. He's dead. Why can't you say it? You don't lose people, Adam. They aren't umbrellas. You love them and then they leave you. They die.'

Maybe she was trying to be helpful. *Face your demons* had always been one of her catchphrases. But Adam felt as if she had kicked him in the gut. As if he were lying on the ground, his intestines spilling about like tagliatelle, his brain close to seizure and in the distance the sound of her sneer. He stood up and walked away.

She didn't call him back and he didn't turn in her direction until he was safely behind the polished cherrywood counter. He should have remembered her tendency to be brutally frank. At times it could be attractive; right now it seemed ugly, almost vindictive. Her head was bent, he noticed, perhaps in remorse? And he was pleased to see the American he had served earlier – who had gone hunting for a meal in Chinatown and now returned – offering her a handkerchief. Adam knew how tenacious Americans could be. Almost as insistent as that little goblin, Mahmoud. Well, he wished her luck with him.

10.30pm

Mahmoud was keeping out of Adam's way. He could tell from the way he moved: short sharp jabs at the till, his elbows and cheekbones prominent, his voice tight and mannered, that he was angry about something. Long before he learnt the vocabulary of whichever country he was in, Mahmoud had taught himself to read bodies. He could spot hostility at a hundred paces; he could tell the difference between the implacable and the pliable; he could pick out chinks of hope. He had seen such chinks in Adam, when he had first starting watching him, when he had been drawn to him as a protector.

Deciding that the best way to pacify him was by looking after his lady friend, Mahmoud hovered behind the cast-iron column at the corner of Stella's sofa. The American had tucked his rejected handkerchief back into his pocket. 'Flew in from Boston yesterday morning,' he was saying. 'Still getting over the jet lag. You a local girl?'

'I only moved in today.'

'Does that make us both new kids on the block?'

She shrugged, but he was not easily discouraged. The leather

147

sighed as he lowered himself onto it. 'I'm staying over at the Crowne Plaza. But they told me this was the best end of town for night life so here I am.' Leaning forward too eagerly, he knocked over her drink. Mahmoud sprang forward to mop it up and felt a small glow of pride when Stella smiled at him.

The Bostonian insisted on buying another, pressed a ten-pound note into Mahmoud's hand and told him to keep the change. Not daring to face Adam's wrath, Mahmoud took some time, furtively pouring a double shot and using the till at the far end of the bar, under cover of one of the waitresses. When he got back, Stella was looking mutinous and the Bostonian disappointed. 'I was kinda hoping you could show me the ropes.'

Mahmoud, considering himself a resident, was anxious to help. 'This is right place!' he said excitedly. 'This is Ropewalks Quarter. You know? Like circus?' In his fantasy, tightropes were webbed across the narrow streets like a cat's cradle; acrobats and trapeze artists swayed high above the ground, balancing their bodies with a confetti of coloured parasols.

The man was impressed. 'No kidding?'

Stella seemed bent on disillusion. 'No,' she said. 'No circus. Just sweat-shops. There were roperies for kitting out the ships, that's all.' She grimaced as she drank, as if the alcohol were purely medicinal. 'Names aren't what they seem, you know. Don't make the mistake of thinking that Hope Street was named after one of the three graces. Mr Hope was just some local landowner. So was Mr Parr, Mr Colquitt, Mr Slater…'

'Paradise also?' said Mahmoud, deflated.

'I don't know about Paradise Street.' Her head lurched forward and her body seemed to double up in spasm.

The American looked anxious. 'Are you okay?'

Her hand over her mouth, she spoke through her fingers. 'Sorry,

I'm not used to this. I've been out of circulation for a while. I spent most of last year in Alderhey Hospital.'

He wriggled away from her as if she were contagious. He forced a smile. 'Nothing serious, I guess? I mean, you look terrific.'

He was being gallant: she was too thin, her nails were bitten to stubs, her cheeks were unnaturally flushed. So were his.

'Don't you know anything?' she said scornfully. 'Alderhey is a children's hospital.'

'Shoot, I'm sorry. No disrespect…' He edged away, backing himself off the sofa, nearly stumbling over Mahmoud in his haste to avoid the difficult or the unpalatable. Not all single women were a breeze to be with.

Mahmoud made the abandoned Stella a formal bow. 'You want to rest in office?' he said.

'In Adam's office?'

He nodded. 'I know combination.'

'Really I should go,' she said. 'I should go back to my apartment.'

He could see the thought of it chilled her: the waiting void, the automated controls, the silence. As she stood up, she staggered a little. Holding her elbow he steered her down the corridor, past the toilets and through the door marked Private.

1.30am

Adam was cashing up. The takings were slightly down on last night, but respectable for the middle of the week. There'd been little trouble: a brief scuffle between some lads who'd had to be led outside like frisky ponies, a noisy domestic, a pair of gay footballers driven away by naïve and flirtatious females. But no serious scenes, no vomit, no complaints of theft or harassment. The last stragglers left quietly, like small children, in search of taxis home. He hadn't noticed Stella's departure. He still felt bitter at her callousness. He

149

hadn't been asking for sympathy, but he hadn't expected such a curt reaction either. What kind of friendship was that?

He dismissed the rest of the staff. Mahmoud, he knew, would be leech-like. He could see him still mopping a patch of floor. He'd have to boot him off the premises and shoo him into the night. However darkly the boy's eyes pleaded, he would *not*, would never, take him home. He counted the coins into the cashbox. He banded the notes, slipped them into envelopes, and carried them to his office. Out of superstition he never switched on the light until all the money was stored in the safe. He had an absurd notion that somebody at street level might peer down through the grating and catch the number of the combination lock. For this reason, also, he changed it every week.

The door of the safe had just swung open and his hand was reaching inside when he heard the movement, saw the shadow stir and rise from the couch. For a moment he froze. He knew managers who kept small revolvers tucked in unlikely places – out of paranoia or bravado. Adam thought it was asking for trouble. Recovering himself, he slammed the safe shut and flicked on the overhead light.

'Jesus!' said Stella. 'You gave me a fright.'

'How the fuck did you get in here?'

'Your boyfriend brought me. To escape the Bostonian. Has he gone yet?'

'Everybody's gone. It's two in the morning. And he's not my boyfriend.'

'Christ, then I must have passed out. I didn't realise…' she frowned, as if trying to remember the blank time she had lost. 'Sorry. I guess I sort of developed the knack – you know, snatching a few hours' sleep here or there on a pull-out bed – when Lucy was in Alderhey.'

'Lucy?'

'My daughter.'

He was tired, confused, his head was buzzing. 'I didn't know you had a daughter.'

'Well I did. Six years ago. I'm sure I sent you a card but you'd probably moved a dozen times already.' She paused. 'And then I didn't. And now I don't.'

Adam felt the knot in his stomach tighten. Tragedy is not exclusive, tragedy casts her net wide. 'I'm so sorry,' he said.

Stella looked around the office: files of orders, a retro Bakelite telephone, a slim silver computer. 'D'you keep any drink in here?'

Adam, who had barely had two pints all night, took a flask of brandy from the bottom drawer of the desk and passed it to her. She pulled him down to sit beside her, took a long swig and then, with her hand gripping his thigh and her eyes fixed on the wall clock, she said 'Leukaemia. At the time I didn't know which was worse: the frantic hoping for a miracle or the days when you simply gave up, resigned yourself. Now I know I'd do anything to be back there again, reading to her, watching her smile, feeding on hope.' She faltered. 'I miss her so much…sometimes I think I can't bear it.'

He placed his hand over hers, remained silent.

She turned towards him. Their faces were now so close he could see the tiny lines of care that hadn't been there, ten, fifteen years ago. 'I am truly sorry,' she said, 'That I upset you before. It was unforgivable. A mixture, I suppose, of too much alcohol and still being so bloody angry. Angry at Lucy's death, at the hypocrisy of people in general and my bloody husband in particular.'

'It isn't fair to blame him,' said Adam. He remembered Nick as a steady dependable type; he remembered being grateful that someone else was taking charge of Stella's mood swings.

She took another long pull at the brandy bottle, but her voice was raw and rasping. 'He stopped sleeping with me, he wouldn't give me another baby. Another baby might have been a donor, could have saved Lucy's life. How can I live with that?'

'Well look at us,' said Adam. 'A pair of celibates.' It was over two years since Ben died and he'd finally got used to it. At first, like Stella, he'd been furious. And furiously promiscuous. Now he was through to the next level and abstinence seemed a whole lot easier. He put his arms around her, let her head droop onto his shoulder, savoured the warmth of another person's flesh.

A small tinkling sound trickled up the corridor. 'Fuck!'

'Is someone trying to break in?'

'I don't know. Look, we've got to get a move on. I have to lock up properly.' He was on his feet, racing ahead. Stella, hobbling on high-heeled sandals, followed.

Mahmoud was sweeping up a shattered wineglass. He smiled uncertainly.

'Okay, that's enough. Let's go.' Adam was exhausted, drained. He'd escort Stella home and then walk up to his flat in Faulkner Square, shaking off Mahmoud on the way. He never used to crave solitude, but times change.

Stella was rummaging in her bag. She noted with contempt two more missed calls from Nick. Then she began to panic. 'Shit. I can't find my keys.'

Adam was ready to set the alarm. Everything was shuttered and silent. Stripes of light from street lamps picked out the sheen of the polished floor, a chrome table leg, a row of clean glasses. Stella emptied her handbag into one of these patches of silver and scrabbled among lipsticks, combs, phone, diary, purse and a small precious folded photo-frame. No keys.

'You had them at the bar when you came in,' said Adam. He

could see them spinning on her finger: the promise of a new life. 'I'm starting over,' she'd said.

'Then we must look,' she commanded.

Lights on again, towels lifted. A torch for the dark recesses beneath the shelving. They found pens, cigarette lighters, coins, but no keys.

'You've been clearing up,' said Stella accusingly to Mahmoud. 'You must have come across them somewhere.'

He spread his hands, shook his head.

'Then they've been stolen. Shit, shit, shit, shit!'

'Don't be crazy. Who would take your keys and leave your cash? Has anyone got a spare set?'

'Only the letting agency. You don't think I'd give Nick the chance to come calling do you? This is a trial separation. I'm supposed to start painting again...'

'Maybe you should go back to him, Stella.'

She scowled. 'I'd rather sleep on the street.' And glanced hopefully down the corridor.

Adam shook his head. 'Sorry, out of bounds.'

She was on her knees, stuffing her belongings into her bag, her shoulders shaking.

'You lost them because you got so lashed, love. I'm sure they'll turn up.'

Mahmoud said suddenly: 'I can help.'

3.00am

Adam and Stella stood holding hands outside her new apartment. She had taken off her sandals in the middle of Duke Street because her feet hurt and they were now dangling from her fingers. The french doors she'd left ajar were fifty feet above their heads. A horizontal metal post, once used to winch goods up to the top floor of the warehouse, thrust itself forward over the balcony. Technically, anyone who could scale the building could climb out along the bar, drop down and enter through the windows.

'This place, I know,' said Mahmoud. 'I sleep here maybe two, three times.'

'I thought all these developments were scally proof.'

Mahmoud looked down modestly. There was little he hadn't experienced in the way of hiding on alarmed premises, boarding boats unseen or clinging to the under-carriage of a train at speed. He had even managed to thwart a pair of sniffer dogs by concealing himself in a container full of lilies. 'In my country,' he said. 'I climb mountains. Very high.'

Stella was impatient. Her first evening alone was now, she felt, at its final ebb. She really couldn't cope with any more of it; she really needed to lie down. She longed for sleep and looked forward to her dreams because Lucy was in them. Actually, of course, as the vicar had said at the funeral, when they had launched hundreds of red balloons heavenwards, Lucy was probably in Paradise.

'Go for it, Mahmoud,' she said.

Adam had dropped Stella's hand and was examining the sheer face of the building, the smooth unbroken pointing. 'Are you crazy? He'll kill himself.'

'Is no problem,' said Mahmoud. He took off his dirty trainers and rolled back his sleeves. Stella saw for the first time the marks etched on his arms: the scars of survival.

'For fuck's sake, Stella! Tell him to stop.'

'I am Spiderman,' Mahmoud called from the top ridge of a ground floor window. He was spread-eagled against the brickwork – more like a fly than a spider – a scrappy dark shape with elongated limbs.

'But Adam, I need to get in. Or I'll collapse. And look how well he's doing, just like the old Milk Tray advert.'

'There's nothing for him to grip, no toe-holds. He'll fall.'

'Dear God,' she said, in a small weary voice, 'I am so tired'.

He grabbed her arm to stop her sinking on to the pavement. 'Look, just forget this escapade. I'm only up the road, in Faulkner Square.' He was still renting. He didn't want to buy. Why commit yourself? He had high ceilings, long windows and a spare room into which he banished clutter. He took a deep breath. 'You'd better come back with me for what's left of the night and we'll sort something out in the morning. I'm sure the keys will turn up.'

Her expression was unreadable, but he heard her whisper: 'Like old times.'

'New times,' he said firmly. He cupped his hands around his mouth and yelled at Mahmoud. 'Come on arselicker. Get down from there. We're all going to my place.'

The fly quivered on its perch. Then, with a mighty leap, it landed joyfully back on the ground.

Rules of the Game

Adrian Reynolds

So you wake up and it wasn't a dream - you did talk and her number's on the flap of the Rizla packet that's poking out of your jeans. The woman in The Peacock you were calling Daryl Henna in your pillow talk before you even spoke. She's working in the day, Skidoo or something, that gallery on the way to Selectadisc, which means you've got hours to research that casual call since you want this one to go right.

You've got to go somewhere, and it can't just be a drink or a meal after the way you joked about dating last night, so you look through *City Lights* and strike out a couple of bands because they've been in the charts already and you know you'll be five years older than most of the audience which makes you almost as old as the group and that just won't do. Which means the only suitable gig - barring Air at Rock City, and the tickets are sold out - is Christ On A Mountainbike, who are admittedly great live but unfortunately look better in cycling shorts than you do. Besides, Mandy might still be selling t-shirts for them and that's a confrontation you could do without this special evening. If she's lived in Nottingham more than six months she'll have seen them once or twice anyway, which also means she's unlikely to be quite so impressed by your being on smoking terms with Dermot the bass player. Over the page then, which is where the fringe events are listed and adding sophistication to your credentials can only be a good thing where Ms. Henna is concerned (but remember - her name's Anne). Alternative Circus is as pricy as it is passé, but elsewhere and

159

cheaper - and nearer your place if we're going to be practical about these things - is a post-Lenny Henry comedian who impressed at least one of the music weeklies with his offhand surrealism and corduroy shirt. Tony Dapper it is then, tickets £7.50 (£6.00 concs), 8.30 meaning 9.30 and a Grolsch in the bar beforehand. But what to wear? The leather's good, and though she's already seen it, a consistent image could suggest a more general self-assurance, but then there's the new hooded top, the G-Force one...these things matter when impressions are formed in a breakbeat barrage of soundbites and samples, and identity - as a caption in the last *i-D* over a distorted photocopy of a French philosopher paraphrased - is a matter of imposing your own signal on everyone else's noise.

Zoe gave the end of the joint her trademark flourish and calmly and deliberately lit it. Anne felt herself tense but was careful to maintain her composure - Zoe had taken to skinning up after what was euphemistically termed the lunch-time rush a few days after Anne had started working at the gallery, and it was now part of what might in others be a routine but in Zoe's case was most definitely a ritual. Anne fidgeted and couldn't help looking to the door, catching Zoe's oblique gaze as her eyes returned to the game of Sonic the Hedgehog that one of the exhibits was playing with itself in the corner. As Zoe passed the joint, Sonic wagged a solemn blue finger and - passionless, pointless, pixel-precise - executed a perfect triple somersault.

'Matt!'

Matt looked up. He'd been circling the square for half-an-hour and was glad of the interruption.

'Haven't seen you in ages, man - what've you been doing?' Clearly it was someone who knew him, but he couldn't work out who. The hair and leggings pointed to one of the skate crew he'd hung round with a couple of months last year, but without a board it was hard to be sure. People change.

'Oh, you know, a few projects ticking away, but nothing bigtime.'

'Still working yeah?'

'Just a couple of days now. Gives me time…' Matt trailed the sentence off with a sweep of his hand.

'Uh-huh.'

'How about you?'

'Still doing the course. Final year now.'

'What about afterwards?'

'Dunno. Figured I'd hang round here a while, see what comes up. You know how it is.'

Matt nodded sympathetically.

'Anyway - got to shoot. Nice seeing you. Give my love to Cass, yeah?'

Matt sat by the fountain and watched the pigeons. Who the fuck was Cass?

It might be good, thought Anne. She'd been a bit drunk last night but Matt didn't seem like most of the jellyheads she'd met lately. A poseur maybe, but that's to be expected in The Peacock and they usually loosen up after a pint and if she remembered not to say anything too pertinent. She'd given him her number and from the way he'd looked at her she guessed he'd be calling tonight. Just as long as he doesn't suggest seeing Christ On A Mountainbike. Ever since her little fling with the bassist, Declan, she hadn't dared to see a local band for fear they might be supporting.

Matt paused as he turned to leave the vegetable aisle. Some reduced peppers had taken his attention, but if he got those he wouldn't be able to afford any cheese and that meant no sandwiches for work. Unless...he performed a rapid calculation. Ditch the yoghurt and the biscuits, or forget the oranges and go for the cheaper of the apples. But then would he still be able to get the peanut butter? His mind raced and he found himself static, with no consciousness of having moved there, in front of a display of tinned peaches, heart skipping at a striplight flicker. He wanted a cigarette.

'Excuse me, I wonder if you could spare a minute to talk. There's a lot of terrible things happening around the world and I'd like to share my feelings about what we all can do.' He was young and he was German and he looked hot in his suit. A badge identified him as Elder Karsten.

Before Anne could say anything, he continued. 'I'm a member of The Church of Jesus Christ of Latter-day Saints. Have you heard of this?' His teeth gleamed white.

'The Mormons?'

'Yes - that is another of our names, but properly we are known as the Latter-day Saints. Most probably you know of us because of our association with polygamy, but that is something that was only practised by a small minority of our members and is no longer a part of our beliefs.' He spoke with weary fluency.

'Pity.'

'Sorry?'

'I said it's a pity. Shouldn't people be allowed to marry if they love each other?'

'Yes, of course. But only one man and one woman. Any more and is...not possible.'

'Why? I can love lots of men.'

'Yes, but there is a difference between loving someone and having a relationship with them.'

162

'Only if you're a hypocrite.'

Elder Karsten looked confused.

Matt watched some of the news – Jordan announcing her engagement to Peter Andre and a reported mass grave in Bosnia, Serbs killed by Croats or Muslims killed by Serbs or something like that - but then Vaughan came round with the Banana Splits video he'd been on about the other night so they watched that for a bit and argued about whether the fourth Split was called Fleegle or Famine, Drooper or Death and then it was time to meet Anne.

He sounded younger on the phone somehow, but funny and unfussed, and only a couple of decibels of anxiety entered his voice when he'd enquired what she was doing that evening. She'd no plans, she said, and left it open to him. The comedian had been on Graham Norton last week, she remembered, wondering why reviewers said post-Lenny Henry when they meant black. He was OK.

Matt hadn't got beyond the label of his Grolsch when the audience were called to see the night's first performer. They finished their drinks and drifted in halfway through what was presumably a satirical song rendered unhearable by fuzz guitar and audience indifference. 'Just what the world needs; a grunge comedian,' Anne grunted. Matt found himself laughing. They sat down.

The song dissolved into feedback and isolated applause. Undeterred, the guitarist launched into his next number, revealing that 'This one's about…' before unleashing another E chord. It must have been about something pretty involved because it was two verses, three choruses and nearly a Bristol Suspension of bridge longer than the first one. It was too noisy to talk, or they didn't want to broach the intimacy of breathing into each other's ears, so they shrugged helplessly and looked at the stage. After a minute they glanced back to one another.

'Isn't that...?' enquired Matt.

'...the guy who plays bass in Christ On A Mountainbike?' said Anne. 'I think so.'

After two more songs he left the stage. They didn't catch his name. Over another Grolsch in the interval they agreed that they didn't like him, and they didn't much like Christ On A Mountainbike either. But at least, said Anne, wrinkling her nose, they're not totally right-on, like Le Tigre, who some guy the other week had wanted her to see. Matt nodded vigorously, adding that he too was sick of the new wave of activist bands which, he improvised, was partly why he was only working three days a week at Selectadisc now. He hinted at discounts if there was anything she particularly wanted at the moment. She smiled and said she'd think about it.

Tony Dapper ambled to the microphone with a shy wave. He began by confusing the venue with the previous night's show in Leicester, and continued to confuse the two gigs at plausibly random intervals in his more obviously scripted material. He'd used the same device with Graham Norton, Anne recalled, pretending that the programme was a South Bank Show devoted to Noel Edmonds. Funnier was a routine about Jimi Hendrix being woken braindead but conscious from a drug coma by S Club 7's manager and offered a job as Lenny Kravitz, which Matt too seemed to like judging by the look on his face, though he hadn't really laughed since Anne's remark earlier. Other jokes concerned the likely whereabouts of Osama bin Laden, ideal methods of birth control, possible ramifications of the Jordan-Andre union, and one contained a knowing reference to ecstasy that made some of the audience whoop like they were on Oprah. For a comedian, Tony Dapper was pretty funny.

'I kept thinking he was going to break into a routine about missing teaspoons and how they all turn up in his sock drawer. It was just...' Matt sucked on his cigarette. 'It was all so safe. Tame, like he knows he's got a good chance of doing his own TV show if he doesn't rock the boat. Get him a catchphrase and a t-shirt and he could be packing the students in for the next two or three years.'

'And only sheep get fleeced, right? You sound jealous.' Anne couldn't work out why Matt was so seemingly distraught at the thought of Tony Dapper's future success. More likely, she speculated, it had less to do with the comedian than the fact that they were sitting in a pub which was going to close in fifteen minutes without either of them having said anything of consequence for - she wasn't sure how long, but they'd met just before eight-thirty and it was now nearly eleven. Maybe consequence wasn't Matt's style - he liked to keep things on a surface level and his surface just went deeper than most. Probably she wouldn't find out unless and until she slept with him, but that wasn't on the agenda yet in any case.

'Jealous no. Pissed off yes - the guy's got a platform and he could be using it, instead of just getting up a rung of the ladder that'll take him to playing golf with Brucie and Branagh.'

'What do you mean, a 'platform'? Because he's black he should be a role model, the Spike Lee of the comedy circuit?' It sounded sharper than Anne had intended, but Matt seemed as intrigued as he was embarrassed.

'That's not what I meant. It's just seeing how the system works. This audience is here now because the guy's been on telly and in the Sunday supplements and the reviewers have said he's good and he's on his way up the food chain growing bigger and more bloated all the time.' Matt grew animated, voice louder and body alert. 'Swelling as he takes in more people until he's a showbiz monster with his own show and tabloids telling you twenty things you never wanted to know about him.'

'Which makes us plankton I suppose.' And me sardonic, thought Anne.

'Something like that. Most TV is aimed at one-celled organisms.' Matt seemed confident now, secure enough in his ability to entertain Anne without monitoring her reactions. He pantomimed a syrupy continuity announcer. 'This programme contains the recommended daily allowance of feel-good sentiment and uncritical acceptance and is guaranteed not to provoke, question, or otherwise disturb your allotted role as passive consumer.'

Anne was amused but unwilling to let Matt get away with his posture, if posture it was. 'And there I was thinking you were just another Viz-reading Banana Splits fan.'

'She's rumbled me.' The experience seemed to be a novelty that Matt enjoyed, and the moment relaxed into a pause they were both comfortable with. 'Listen -'

Anne raised her watch before he could say anything. 'I'll have to go now. The last bus. Give me a call at the weekend, yeah?'

Matt paused for a moment. 'Yeah.'

So you wake up and you feel like checking the curtains to see if the birds are singing and you wonder why you're in a good mood and you remember last night and grin a big shit-eating grin at yourself in the mirror for being so corny but loving it all the same. And even though reality's intruded by the time you've organised some toast it's still good to start the day on a high. You'll meet again at the weekend by the sound of things and probably get drunk and confess that you do in fact like Le Tigre it's just the fans can get a bit earnest you know and you'll both nod and laugh the way people do when they really understand each other and maybe you'll end up in bed which means you'd better do some tidying up before Friday night. You hope you didn't seem too predictable because some of the conversation you came out with was pretty familiar but they're probably thinking the same thing about themselves but you got on and that's the important thing and anyway it's always like that the first time you meet someone. It went pretty well in the end then. Or maybe it was the drink. Either way, it could have been a lot worse. You could have been wasting another evening with the bassist out of Christ On A Mountainbike.

Part II

This Could Be Anywhere

Pig, Who?
Penny Feeny

I shouldn't of told him about the baby. I should of kept my lip buttoned. We had this English teacher at school, used big words all the time, used to shake her head at me and say: You always embellish so, Vicki. But it's not like I can't tell the difference between the truth and a lie. It's just sometimes a story needs helping along, a little push to make it run smoother, and that's what I'm good at. But every now and again, I s'pose, I push a bit too hard and it starts to get out of control. That's how it was with Jonathan really.

Out of the blue he come up to me when I'm sitting on the wall, banging my heels against the bricks in a fury and bawling. I don't recognise him at first. People look different in daylight. He takes a handkerchief out of the top pocket of his suit jacket and offers it to me. I always thought them hankies sticking up like flags was just for show, same as the tie he's got round his neck. You can't imagine people like him ever needing to blow their noses. Even with his mates he's a bit of a stuffed shirt, Jonathan. He don't laugh much at jokes and when they're nudging him to have another, he looks solemn and puts his hand over the top of the glass.

That's how I know him, from the bar. They come for drinks after work, settling on high stools or low sofas like a flock of starlings, and sometimes they stay half the night like they've got nothing to go home for. That's their lives really: work, drink, perch on the wire, back to work again. It's perfectly respectable, our place, not lap-dancing or anything. I was a proper waitress, all rigged out

173

in black. Customers could slip a tip into my apron pocket but if they tried to slip their hands anywhere else, know what I mean, they'd be for it.

Well Vicki, says Jonathan. What's this all about?

I'm impressed he's remembered my name till I see him looking at my badge. Should of thrown it back in the Rottweiler's face along with everything else. I been sacked, I tell him.

Oh, I'm sorry.

I've noticed this about him before, how polite he is. Some of them got no manners. They grab at your skirt and call you a dozy sow and pretend they're going to vomit over your shoes when they've had a skinful. That's why I always wear trainers. But Jonathan always says please and thank-you and would you mind. Never seems to get those dark patches of sweat under his armpits when he takes his jacket off. Keeps his fingernails clean.

While I'm wiping my eyes he sits himself on the wall beside me.

Can they do that?

We're only casual labour. They can do what they bloody want.

Surely there's a reason?

I got in a bit late.

People are staring at us curiously as they pass by, as if they think he's the one making me cry. The Rottweiler yelled at me about my bad time-keeping like it was a crime against nature – though she's always making us stay on and clear up for no extra.

Is that all?

Well it sounds feeble, don't it? Needs a push. I can't help it, I explain. It's cos I've been feeling sick. Cos I'm pregnant. That's the real reason they don't want me.

He frowns. I didn't think they could do that. Then he stands up and brushes off his legs carefully. He's looking down on me again. His eyes are a bit close together, but he has a nice firm jaw, very smooth. He's probably rich enough to pay a barber every morning to give him that clean-cut look. Fancy aftershave of course. Not like the cats' piss that some lads wear. Everything about him is expensive. I'm not used to a man like this taking my side. I don't want him to go.

Fresh tears come easy. I don't know what I'm going to do, I wail. Me mam threw me out when she heard about the baby. I'm s'pose to be moving into me own place but now I int got enough for the deposit. Will he fall for it? Will he offer to fork out the difference? A hundred quid's nothing to him and he was quite a fair tipper when I'd bring the drinks over. Not exactly generous, mind – probably never got drunk enough – but fair. Sometimes I even seen him digging in his pocket for change for the Big Issue.

So you're telling me you've no home, no job and you're pregnant?

Yes.

How old are you, Vicki?

Nineteen.

It's six o'clock on a summer evening and everyone else has somewhere to go. I wonder is he sizing me up? How's he going to walk off now? Make him look like a right callous bastard won't it, if all he leaves me with is one crumpled snotty hanky.

He pats his black leather executive briefcase. Do you like Dover sole?

Now I don't reckon I ever had Dover sole, not unless you can get it in batter down the chippy and I'm wondering what kind of man carries a wet fish around in his briefcase. Almost sends me running but, like I said, I never been this close to money before.

'S allright.

Why don't you come and have supper with me? Maybe I can help you work something out – even talk to your mother for you.

No, no, please don't. She's got this awful violent boyfriend. What else could I say? That's the trouble with embellishment, one little piece of decoration, like a nice ferny frond or a scattering of flower petals, leads to another. Suddenly you've planted a whole fucking garden and it's grown into a jungle with no way out.

Jonathan's house is kind of like Jonathan, tall and narrow and sober. The roof slopes the way his shoulders do, stone lintels overhang the windows like his eyebrows. The kitchen is all smooth stainless steel, with nothing out of place – not even a knife or a pepper-pot. Running down the middle of it is this long marble table, bit like a mortuary slab, and he slaps the dead sole down on it. Then he goes over to an enormous fridge and gets out two beers and it's so like one of those adverts off the telly I'm thinking I've walked into a dream.

I take the beer into his living room, which isn't my idea of cosy. The floor is polished wood but it clatters when I walk on it, and when I sit on the black leather sofa it squeaks like a kitten you're stroking the wrong way. All these protesting noises AND it feels lonely. It feels as if someone has taken away all the comfy old chairs and the potted plants and the family photos and just left hard black surfaces. He's not really living here, only camping. The books look like they've been bought to fill a space and most of the CDs I int even heard of. The only ornaments are a dish of grey pebbles and a weird face mask with all sorts of patterns carved into it, like voodoo or black magic. For one scary moment I think Christ, he's not grinding his knife blade to fillet the fish. He's going to cut me open because he wants my blood or my non-existent foetus for some kind of ritual. I watch too many horror films, me. He's an accountant for fucksake.

He comes to find me and sees me looking at the awful thing and spits sharp as a needle, Don't touch that.

Seems it's some ancient fertility icon, very valuable but brittle as matchsticks. When I ask what it's doing in his lounge he just says, Let's eat now.

Well he's got no ketchup but the wine's nice, cool and fruity like Jonathan's voice. He's trying to explain the sort of work he does. Men always think you should be interested in their work because it makes them feel important, but I'm only half-concentrating. When he talks about liquidation I imagine his white and silver kitchen as a giant iceberg melting all around us. And when he talks about receivership I think for a moment he's just another con been handling stolen goods. When he says bankrupt, I finally get the picture. No money, that's something I know about.

Let me get this straight. You're sorting all these firms that have gone bust?

Yes.

So how d'you get paid?

He smiles and tries to explain, because it's clear as water the money is rolling in. I get bored before he's finished but I get the picture right enough. He's just a high-class bailiff — but, shit, what does it matter if he can afford a TV screen as wide as this one.

Vicki, he says and shows all his teeth. You're like a breath of fresh air.

I spin out the dinner as long as I can because I don't know what's going to happen next, whether I can face going back to his squeaky lounge with the creepy mask or whether I want him to jump me or whether I'd feel insulted if he didn't. Of course in the bar you flirt a bit, specially if it's going to up your tips, but you don't mean it. Now he's looking nervous too. He's not done this before, not with someone like me. Does he think I play by different rules?

I think I ought to go, I say.

.

Where?

I can go to me mate, Shell's. She'll let me kip on her floor.

He's looking straight at me with his narrow eyes, but I can't read the expression in them. I've two spare bedrooms here, he says. Might be more comfortable for you.

Pig in clover, that's what I am. Can't believe my luck. I always fancied a sugar daddy and here he is. My own room, nice big bed, clean white sheets, and no strings attached. Every morning I wake up, stretch, think I've died and gone to heaven. I can hear the cleaning woman downstairs polishing them wooden floors but she's foreign, don't speak much English, so I lie here and ignore her. Shell wouldn't believe me at first, said I was having her on. Whaddya mean, lodger? she snorted. You paying rent? You're his bloody tart.

I don't bother to argue. I know I'm lucky. You don't often get to see into people's lives like this. I mean, I could of served him drinks every day for ten years – instead of just six months – and still not know nothing except the cut of his suit. Now I know he lives alone in a swanky town house and plays classical music while he potters about cooking gourmet meals. I nod my head and listen carefully when he goes on about stuff at work and I always make the coffee and wash the pans. He likes to hear me singing even though he don't know the songs and I reckon he appreciates having a bit of life in his frigid old house.

We're not like a couple or anything. We don't go out together. Some evenings he goes off on these corporate dos – or maybe even to see a film – what would I know? He won't take me back to the bar neither, though I'd give anything to see the Rottweiler's face when I walk in on his arm. Says it's cos I shouldn't be drinking. Says someone has to keep an eye on me and look after the welfare of the baby. Since that first meal he won't offer me no more wine and no way will he let me smoke. Like he's my dad or something. He says I shouldn't stay out so late with Shell, but I don't reckon it's any of his business.

When I get back from a club night I always take my shoes off on the doorstep so's I don't disturb him, but one time he's waiting up for me. Usually the house is dead quiet so at first I think I'm hearing a burglar prowl around on the creaky floorboards. Then I realise it's Jonathan standing in the hallway. The air's hot as hell's kitchen and he's only wearing a pair of pyjama bottoms but his arms are folded tight across his chest and he's frowning.

He almost shouts at me, Where have you been?

I shrug. I been with Shell. Dancing.

Do you realise what time it is?

What?

I want you in by midnight in future.

What! Who the fuck does he think he is?

This is my house, Vicki. I make the rules. If you don't like them you can go.

I can feel the anger boiling up inside when he says, You should listen to me you know. Someone has to protect your health and the future of your baby.

I lose my rag easy. I lunge at him but he grabs my wrist. And then it happens so quickly we neither of us have time to stop it. Fact is, I'm giddy with the drink and he's not had a sniff of nothing for months. One minute he's pinning my hands behind my back and the next I'm flat on his leather sofa with my vest pushed up to my neck and my thong snapped round my ankles. I wouldn't call it rape though. In about five seconds he's lying limp, a dead weight on top of me.

Christ, Vicki, he says. I'm sorry.

It's okay.

I really didn't intend…

I said it's okay.

I push him away and take the rest of my clothes off properly. The room's in darkness but there's enough street light coming through his venetian blinds to make stripes on my skin. I lift the voodoo mask off its hook and hold it in front of my face. Then I pace up and down and growl like I'm a tiger and I'm going to pounce on him. And this time he don't tell me I shouldn't be touching it. He's staring at me like he's trapped in a hole. Makes me feel powerful when his eyes roll and his cock rises. I know I'm fit, I'm not one of them has everything fake. Anyway, it had to happen, right? You don't get a feller and a girl together in the same house without them ending up shagging. Let him think he was a gentleman for waiting, and I can think I'm no whore for the same reason.

I'm pleased really that we done it, makes me feel I've more of a right to be living here. (Though we still keep to our own rooms. I don't care to lie next to someone else sweating all night long.) He's not a great fuck, I have to say. He's a bit flabby. Really I prefer a man to be dead hard all over, like my ex was – but he used to work out and, to be honest, he'd rough me up sometimes too. Jonathan don't even scratch with his toenails or scrape my face with his stubble. He's soft as a baby and it's funny to think people are queuing up in front of him all day long, in tears probably, begging him not to take their family heirlooms or to leave them a piece of machinery so they can start a new factory going again. Would they dry their eyes, would it give them a laugh if I was to tell them, whisper in their ears, that he was a bit of a wimp in bed?

Vick, says Shell when I show her the little stick I just weed over. You are such a stupid dork.

See, Jonathan's been a bit casual with the condoms. Like he'd try to remember to use them in case I'd got Aids or something, but you could see he felt really awkward. Like, if I'm clean enough to live in his perfect house and clean enough for him to stick his tongue down my throat then I should be clean enough for his precious unsheathed dick. And of course contraception isn't an issue. For him. Which is why I'm now up shit creek and Shell's telling me it's way too late to take the morning-after pill.

So d'you think I oughta tell him?

The flame flares up so high from her lighter I think it's going to singe her eyelashes.

No way! Just get rid of it and say you lost it. That's what you was going to do all along, right?

Somehow it's different now, though. Now that there actually is something growing inside me. Now that the smell of alcohol makes me retch and the first fag of the day tastes like cinders. And I start to think, whey hey, it wouldn't be so bad for a kid to have a dad like Jonathan. Imagine how things might of turned out if my dad had been an accountant instead of a disappearing-into-the-distance lorry driver. I could get my kid such a cool buggy he'd think he was riding in a frigging chariot. And he'd have his own nursery all done out for him, posh.

Then I get doubts. Like s'pose I lose my figure? And how am I going to explain? What if he don't believe me? We'll have to take them DNA tests and everything. And what do I know about him anyway? Why hasn't he had kids before? He's over forty for Godsake. Maybe he has one of them gruesome diseases that get passed on. Or worse. Don't dare tell Shell this, but I found two women's dresses hanging up behind his fitted sliding doors. Stashed away beneath a load of suits like a guilty secret. He don't know I spotted them. How do I know he int a sodding transvestite, jerking

181

off into a pair of satin knickers? Is that the kind of person I want to be the father of my kid?

I'm so mixed up I don't know what to think. Fact is, I quite like him. I wouldn't ever of said that I fancied him – he's too old for one thing – but it isn't just the money makes him smell nice. He's grateful to me. He don't just roll over and snore after a shag. He gasps a bit, but even when he's short of breath he'll say thank-you. Now I'm not pretending I want to spend the rest of my life with him, but I reckon we can work something out. And anyway, as Shell says, there's a few weeks to go yet. Loads of pregnancies don't amount to nothing. I could be bleeding again soon enough. Something always turns up – usually when you least expect it.

Most definitely I am not expecting HER. I been out to do a bit of shopping – well, pricing really. And I been looking at some travel brochures, hoping maybe I could persuade him to take me on a nice trip. To the sea, I think, before I'm too fat to look good in a bikini. Ibiza's wicked, Shell says, or Majorca. But to be honest, Jonathan isn't the party type. It's a shame he's not into dancing cos there's nothing like spinning around a dance floor to make you forget your troubles. So, anyway, I got my arms full of these brochures, colours so wild they do your head in, and I skip along to the kitchen, and she's hovering there like a ghost. Actually she's more like Morticia from the Addams Family, tall and beaky and dressed in black. She has heavy black hair too and a thin face and a cruel mouth and she's looking at me as if I'm a half-dead bird the cat's brought in.

Good afternoon, she says like ice cracking.

I let them spill at my feet, all those pictures of sunny skies and jazzy umbrellas and tanned bodies glistening with oil. Who the hell are you?

I'm Francine. You must be Vicki.

Francine who?

Jonathan's wife.

I didn't even know he had a fucking wife. Never mentioned her. Never got a call from her. I never even seen a photo – though he don't have pictures of people on his walls, only buildings. Or dead things like rocks and stones. What kind of marriage is it if there's no trace of her in the house except maybe them two dresses I was wondering about? And I know for a fact he hadn't had sex for months, he was gagging for it.

Frankie and Johnnie, I snort. I can't help it, makes me laugh.

She raises an eyebrow. She's plucked them both so fine they're like two metal hoops and her eyes are the balls you want to sock right through them.

You divorced then?

We've been having a trial separation. My plane was early for once.

She pulls out a chair and sits down, crossing her legs so that her foot bounces gently above the floor. I never seen shoes with such pointy toes. I wonder how she can hardly walk in them, but she's the type probably travels everywhere by taxi.

I suppose, she drawls very slowly in her funny accent. I suppose it's fairly obvious what he sees in you.

It's obvious all right. Her skin is dry and papery, her make-up is cracking round her nose and mouth. If she was any thinner you'd try to hang your coat on her.

I'm not going to hang around waiting for a showdown. He's sure got some explaining to do but she can have first listen. So I leave her there, in what used to be her kitchen, where I bet she never lifted a finger while he faffed about grinding his spices and chopping his herbs. I go to my own room and slam my fists into the pillow, wishing it could be her smug face. I'm more than mad, I'm spitting feathers cos of the way he lied. Why couldn't he of said he was separated? And how did she know about me? He must of told her, he must of been sending her emails all along. What does that make me? Some stupid stunt he's trying to pull?

I hear him come in, all unsuspecting, and part of me wants to fling myself onto him, wind myself around him like a cat, lick his ear and whisper a warning. The rest of me wants to cut his balls off. I pick up my phone and start to text Shell but I know she'll only come back with a load of questions I can't answer yet and an I-told-U-so. I'm waiting for the sounds of a row, him growling, her snarling, maybe a nice piece of china smashed. But nothing. I slink back down the stairs. Seems a bit too quiet to me. S'pose I walk in and find them snogging each other?

They're sitting at opposite ends of the long marble table. I could jump up and do a dance number or sashay down the middle like it was a catwalk and I wouldn't feel any more stupid than I already do. My tits are firm, my stomach's still flat as a board and I been hours on the sunbeds so I should feel well superior to the two of them hunched up like a pair of black crows. But I am dead nervous and I've this awful sinking feeling inside, like the first time I came here and heard him sharpening his knife. There's plenty of room on that table top for a person to be pinned down, sliced open and sacrificed.

Frankie is right pissed off, I can tell. What were you thinking of Jonathan? she says now. Or should I allow you some higher motive? You fancied yourself as pig male Ian perhaps?

For Godsake, Francine.

Why won't he stand up for himself? Pig, who? I ask and she honks with laughter. Why didn't you tell me about her? I shout as his head sinks further into his collar and his fingers tug at his tie, trying to loosen the knot round his neck.

He groans. I was going to but we still had a lot to sort out. She's been working in New York for a year. She's been having an affair with a colleague. They're both glaring at each other. I thought the marriage was finished.

Jonathan, says the ice-queen, you're lying.

Why should I waste my time listening to this crap? I don't care that I got no shoes on. The pavement will be warm from the heat of the day. I'll go and find Shell and then we'll find ourselves a couple of lads. I'll go for vodka I think, force it down. Vodka don't make you as sick as some of them other spirits. And I am going to get truly bladdered.

I stay away a few days just to give him a fright like the one I got. I won't answer his calls or any of his texts, though he keeps writing he needs to talk. Shell's always said she don't know what I see in Jonathan. Says I should make as much dosh from him as I can and then get out fast. Now I'm beginning to think she's right. I don't know what I'm after anymore. I thought I wanted a sugar daddy who'd be good to me and treat me like I was someone special. It's nice that, when someone cares about you. For three months everything's been clean and simple but now it's all tangled up. I wish I'd not carried on with all the baby nonsense. I wish I'd not got us into such a fucking mess.

When I do go back he's still out at work so I stomp around his living room with the telly on loud – MTV because I need a good thump of music. I want to imagine I'm inside that television set myself, singing and dancing. I don't hear him come in and when he pokes his head round the door, I pretend I int seen him and he goes off to get changed. When he comes down again he's still damp from the shower, looks like he's been left out in the rain, his casual clothes are a joke. And why did I ever think he had a nice face? He's a rat, pointed twitchy nose, close-set beady eyes, sharp teeth. And I thought I liked the fella. I really did. I thought he was kind and classy and all the time he's as much of a bastard liar as the rest of them.

Look Vicki, he says. I'm sorry about Francine. I mean, about her turning up so suddenly like that. I should have warned you.

I shake my head and shrug my shoulders, like I don't care.

He sits beside me on the sofa and flicks the mute button on the remote so the presenters are putting on silly faces and mouthing at us with no sound coming out. I pull up my knees and hang onto my toes and move away from him. I don't want his leathery old hand creeping up my leg no more. But he don't even try to touch me. Look here, he says. I think perhaps things went too far between us. I took advantage of you to get back at Francine and I shouldn't have. I'm sorry.

You two back in the sack then?

He coughs. We've been doing some hard talking. We're going to give our relationship another try.

Now I've blown it. Shouldn't of gone off in a temper like that. I eye him bitterly. Oh nice one. Have your fun and toss me out.

No Vicki. That's what I want to explain. You're welcome to stay.

Is he some kind of perv or what? Does he really think I'm going to crawl into bed with him and his skeleton wife so they can get off on a bit of young flesh?

Why?

You still need a room, don't you? And Francine still has business to wind up in New York so she'll hardly be here. Later on…

Yeah?

After you've had the baby. I mean, you'll want to get another job and perhaps move in with a friend… He runs his hand over his hair which is slicked back close to his scalp. He looks embarrassed and I think how tough and mean he has to be at work and I think how he's got a wife like a witch and a house that's black and white and dead as a photograph and I'm pleased I can still make him squirm. You see, he carries on. We've talked it over and what we'd like, Francine and I, is to adopt your baby.

My mouth falls open, silent as the girl on the telly. Don't know whether to laugh or scream. A baby in this place? With those two? They wouldn't even know which end was which. She might break a fingernail poking a bottle between its gums. He'd get dribbles down his Armani ties. Makes sense now though. All them lectures about looking after myself, not smoking, not drinking, not staying out late. Bloody miracle he didn't insist on coming to the quack with me. He says they don't know why they couldn't have kids of their own, though it's mighty clear to me. Probably int even a woman, that Frankie of his, mincing about on her high heels. Probably not got no sex organs.

It caused problems in our marriage, he says. And a great deal of stress for both of us. It was one of the reasons we decided to separate, why she transferred to New York. We've looked into adoption of course. And surrogacy, which is easier in the States but still a minefield. And then you turned up...

You never gave a shit about me! I was just a fucking incubator.

No of course not. His fingers are fluttering all over the place. You're a sweet girl, Vicki, and I'm sure you'll have a delightful baby. Bouncy and beautiful just like you.

I think I'm going to puke. You don't know nothing about me. Like it turns out I didn't know nothing about you.

In my job you learn to become a good judge of character.

Yeah right. And I thought all you did was shift columns of numbers around and trample poor sods into the ground. In bar work you get to be a judge of character too. I know a fucking wanker when I see one.

Dear girl, calm down.

And anyway, how d'you know what my baby's dad is like? Tell me that. How d'you know he int no thieving junkie psycho rapist?

He clears his throat and his voice gets even more pompous. Well, I admit we've had considerable discussion on the subject, Francine and I. Obviously we'd like some assurances from you before we go ahead. And possibly the father may need to be consulted – but that's up to you, of course.

I keep quiet. It's not often that I'm struck dumb but he's done it. I feel as if the skin is stretched tight across my cheekbones like a mask, his mask with all the carvings that's staring at us. Fertility icon my arse. Wish to hell I'd smashed the bloody thing.

This is the way it would work, he says to the window because I won't look him in the eye. I will take care of you until the child is born. We will then begin the adoption process – and let you have visiting rights of course if you want them. Naturally we still have to work out the figures.

Shell would have focussed on the money. She'd of asked him what he had in mind and doubled it. She's gonna be mad with me, Shell, when she knows what I done. Trouble is, I don't trust him anymore.

She'd have everything she needs, he goes on. She'd be very comfortably provided for. You know that. After all, I've looked after you pretty well haven't I?

What the fuck makes you think I'm having a girl? Can't wait to shag her too?

If he was anyone else he would of hit me and I would of deserved it. I know that. I start to cry and he backs away, don't pass me his hanky this time.

He has his hand on the doorknob, but before he goes, he says: Clearly you get pregnant easily, Vicki. And you'll have other children. This is a good offer and I hope you'll be sensible enough to think it over.

I'm back at me mam's. She's okay that way, Mam, lets me kip at home for a bit in between boyfriends. She has about three different jobs so she's not in much. I can snuggle down on the couch with a pack of Marlboros and a pile of catalogues and no-one going to tell me to keep my feet on the floor. And she don't know what Shell knows neither, so she don't go whinging on about how I could of made a mint and am I a crazy bitch or what?

I tell you, I learned my lesson in that Hammer House of Horror. Everybody's after something, but they got some nerve, that Frankie and Johnny. They're so busy making money and calling the shots and turning everything into an object to stick on a wall, they think they can take whatever they want. They got to think again. The way I see it, I'm well off out of it even if I am still signing on. Shan't be looking for work just yet, not till I feel a bit stronger. Right now I feel hollow and fragile inside like an egg that's been blown – or scraped out with a spoon. No regrets though.

Wings of a Dove
Andrew Parker

You are sitting in the Hare and Hounds with Russell and Rosalind. It's a mild Thursday evening in the merry month of May and the pub is slowly filling up with the same old faces. It also happens to be a special occasion of sorts, for on this day Rosalind has reached the milestone of her twenty-fifth year on the planet; a magical quarter-of-a-century of living. Raise trumpets – cue fanfare. For you, that particular milestone - more like millstone- passed by unnoticed by all and sundry, but it's different for girls and they like to celebrate such tripe accordingly. So Russell has splashed out and bought her – undoubtedly at her request – a girl's best friend (simple setting, plain gold band) which she can't help but flash for the benefit of surrounding females who mince past jealously. But for crying our loud, never have you seen a more obvious created diamond in all your life, for if this monster rock were kosher it would be a veritable *Cullinan*. The thing's got zirconia written all over it, but who cares? Rosalind is happy with it and to that end, it serves its purpose.

But you can't help wondering why it's just three of you at this intimate get-together. Surely Rosalind's mates will soon turn up rat-arsed and falling over themselves but no, you're informed categorically to the contrary; it's just the one two three of you. Being the suspicious sort, and half the time bordering on the paranoiacal, you just can't help wondering why that might be. There's normally a big gang of you whenever there's a sesh up at the *'aries;* why would these two orchestrate it otherwise? And now you come to think of it, they do seem unusually nervous about something; they've each quashed three bottles of beer to your one and Rosalind is already at the bar ordering their fourth. Mmm.

So with Rosalind in splendid isolation over at the mock-mahogany counter top, Russell leans over your table – left eyebrow debonairly raised – and makes a request of your services that in a million years you did not expect to hear.

'Hey Lucas,' he whispers matter-of-factly, 'You up for a threesome with me and her, or what?'

If you were hooked up to an electrocardiograph, a nurse would be running around hysterically shouting 'Tachy at one-eighty, call the crash team, call the crash team!' but as it happens, you're just quietly sitting in your local with your long-standing friend and his bird whom you now see in a profoundly different light. Your pulse is going hammer and tongs, you can feel sweat beading on your forehead, and you're dumbstruck to the highest attainable degree. It takes a while to process his request.

'What?- us, but- where though – the three of us, like…' you bumble.

'Yeah. She's up for it. She suggested it. For her birthday, like.'

You realise you've got to make a decision one way or the other before Rosalind gets back from being served. You glance over at her and she's looking back at you with enormous belladonna fuck-me eyes. If it were just you and her, no problemo. She's blonde, well built, gorgeous enough, in fact for the couple of years she's been around you've always quite surreptitiously fancied her. But with Russell there too, in the same room, it's not a roll-in-the-hay situation you look upon with any relish. The thing is, and you've thought about this before, you don't ever want to be in the same room as another man's erection. No way José. You don't want to be in the same fucking *street* as another man's orgasm, and whilst you're on the subject of all thing erectile, you doubt you could even get *good wood* with a naked male in close proximity, especially one you've known since childhood. In all matters three-way, you're positively *Virgo Intacta*. If you were to be the minority sex in such a deal, that would be a different matter entirely. Rock 'n' roll and all that. But as the offer stands, you just can't see yourself accepting. You think about suggesting a conventional twosome, just you and her like, but you don't want to hurt Russell's feelings. Then Rosalind comes back from the bar wearing an optimistic smirk across her birthday face and she wants a yay or a nay in response to her/their generous offer.

'Well?' she says, sitting down. You're relieved to see she's suitably embarrassed, and at the same time lustfully flushed across her ample cleavage.

'Erm, well, I'll just go to the bog,' you spout yellowy, and retire to the seclusion of the gents for a more thorough consideration. Your reluctance is understandable: a *partie a trois* needs thinking about properly; it's no use jumping in feet first without your wellies on when you don't know what you're jumping into. That way anything could happen, all manner of problems could arise, people could get hurt, friendships and relationships might irretrievably capsize. But on the other hand, you tell yourself whilst making use of the slash-catcher, a *soixante-neuf* with Rosalind would really make your day, even though it's a *partie double* she's drooling after. Oh *baise-moi*, the endless possibilities!

As you zip up your fly, in walks the local dealer in all things euphoriant, aptly nicknamed 'The Borg' (resistance is futile) by some wit of a Trekkie. This is a man who for some years has kept you well supplied with an unlimited crop of cannabis; your regular drug of choice. It's this ability to please that makes him a true friend and confidant to much of the town's pot-smoking populate.

Even during periods of drought he has unfailingly come up with the goods; a most reliable connection. As you greet him he holds his hand out flat.

'Alright Lucas,' he says, 'Have a dekko at that.'

On the palm of that upturned hand lays a beige tablet with a bird of the ornithological variety deeply embossed into one side. For a second you can't quite believe what you are seeing, can't quite believe your luck because for you, this is a strike of eureka proportions. You ask him if that's what you think it is.

'Dove,' he states emphatically. 'Twenty-five nicker. Mates' rates.'

Now this is a real turn-up for the books. Last time you saw The Borg you had asked him to keep his eyes peeled for just this very item. He had laughed in your face when you told him you'd never taken ecstasy before, but he had promised he'd do his utmost to 'sort you out'. Pure unspiked MDMA is a hard commodity to come by at the best of times, and what an opportune moment to be offered it! This could be just what the doctor ordered: an aphrodisiac, an anxiolytic, an antidepressant, and a restorative wonder drug stroke potential dick-stiffener all rolled into one. A transaction is made; you buy at the index-linked asking price. The felonious acquisition goes under your tongue and leaving The Borg in the bog, you make your way back to Troilis and Cressida having had your decision made for you.

You sit back down at the table; they are all ears. You take a swig of flat beer and your pill disappears stomachwards. With a stealthy flourish, you actually wish the fucker Godspeed. Then your eyes are met with a scene effused with silent dialogue as the aforementioned duo apprehensively await your verdict.

'What the hell,' you say. 'Nothing ventured.' And with those five words you officialize the proposed soirée. Everybody goes crimson with the finality of your pronouncement and slump eyes-down into their beer. It's a goer then, and all you can do is hope against hope that the Dove you've just let loose brings you some lasting internal peace; forget the fucking olive branch.

During the next thirty minutes or thereabouts, the methylene dioxymethamphetamine plays merry hell with most of the delicate neurotransmitter systems in your brain: noradrenaline, serotonin, phenylethylamine, in fact every one of the aromatic amines; Ecstasy intoxication renders these brittle mechanisms *kaput*. But its primary action, and the effect everyone raves after, is its ability to block the re-uptake mechanism of dopaminergic neurons, thus increasing *five-fold* the amount of circulating dopamine in the cerebral cortex and the reticular activating system. Mamma Mia! It's like taking a shower with the plug left in the bath; you end up knee-deep in your own dirty water.

So half-an-hour passes; you feel yourself coming up good-style on the Dove. Whereas Russell and Rosalind have understandably become increasingly aloof as the evening progresses, you find yourself seething with nothing less than humanity-embracing benevolence. Every cell in your throbbing body seems to be perfused with joy and happiness; felicity has somehow become an intrinsic bodily component. You are surer than you've ever been about anything, that everything, no matter what, will turn out all right in the end. And it's at the moment of idealistic realization that the formerly silent jukebox suddenly kicks in with *Solsbury Hill* by Peter Gabriel.

That staccato three-note intro merging seamlessly into that nostalgic classical guitar signature! That oh-so-irresistible windy bass drum! That slightly overeager single maraca accompaniment! And then, twelve bars in, when the flautist pipes up with his evocative four-note refrain and Gabriel begins his archangelic statement…Enough! You're already up and dancing, right there in the middle of the Hare and Hounds to the complete astonishment of your co-hosts as well as the other disbelieving patrons.

What exactly is it you're feeling? Some paradoxical compulsion to get down and boogie? An overwhelming urge to move synchronously with the orphean music? Who gives a monkeys! It feels about the best you've ever felt with knobs on. That impossibly mellifluous sound flooding into your body, seemingly through every orifice and pore; it can only be described as a libidinous sonic caress. And an *orange* sonic caress at that, for the music, as strange as it seems, has developed a very definite technicoloured tactility. You're hearing in *colour*! You've become a synaesthete of Olympian stature and you're odds-on favourite to collect gold. Just hope you're not selected for a random drug test.

You hear somebody say 'fucker's as mad as a box of frogs' and images of said amphibi spontaneously zip through your mercurial id, only serving to elevate you even further. Such lovely green and slimy creatures you think, the sheer frogginess of them all! But if your smile gets any wider you surmise your face might split open right across the front because there's no real merriment in that facial expression, no siree. And on top of that you're dancing on the spot like a madman, and that's the sort of vigorous exercise that just can't be healthy in a normally staid young man like yourself. You're about ninety seconds into your impromptu *Solsbury Hill* quickstep when Russell and Rosalind intervene, as is the duty of friends to do so in such circumstances. Their part in the rescue effort involves each grabbing hold of a flailing upper limb, restraining you as best they can whilst you remonstrate like a spoilt brat and, erm, frogmarching you out of the pub to the dying strains of the ex-Genesis frontman.

'Fucker's enriched with social venom.' Rosalind observes.

'What -'

'Vitamin E,' she says. 'Look at the size of his pupils. He's on one.'

'That...fucking Borg!' Russell expounds astutely. He peers directly into your eyes and confirms the diagnosis. Heavens to Murgatroyd; it's still relatively light outside and your pupils are fixed and dilated. Not that you have any inkling whatsoever about your optical mydriasis; all you can do is continue to strut your funky stuff right there in the street. Even the traffic on Liverpool Road throbs just at that specific beat you need to dance along with. And you are tuned into that transcendental tempo so emphatically that you want to dance along with it forever. You've hit upon the very frequency of the universe and nothing is going to stop you surfing the crest of that particular wavelength. You've got a feeling you might just be the Resurrection, but in the meantime your brain chemistry is being irreparably crucified.

All this dereliction can only mean one thing; you know it, Russell knows it, and Rosalind knows it too. She's got her knickers in a twist and looks about as happy as a convent girl with flat batteries, which isn't that far from the actual truth. It's you the blame should fall upon because it's you who's put the kibosh on her triplicate birthday extravaganza. This potential threesome has degenerated, at least for you, into a lonesome onesome.

Far from humanity-embracing benevolence, what you are looking at now is a holocaust-calibre depression deeper even than Larkin's coastal shelf. You are dopamine-depleted to near insentient levels and it's taking all your remaining spatio-temporal capacities just to establish your exact whereabouts, of which you have no fucking idea. But after a minute, you pinpoint your location. You're on the couch, Russell and Rosalind's, and after squinting at your watch for a further minute you verify it's the middle of the next day after the night before. You presume they've upped and gone to work; work being an activity you've long since eliminated from your day-to-day routine. You try to right yourself but find you can hardly move, let alone sit upright. And on top of the catatonic stupor, it seems rigor mortis has set in just for the hell of it. The only physical characteristic you're acutely aware of is a priapic hard-on of hypotension-inducing magnitude, which isn't that unusual in itself, except for the fact you're still fully clothed and the denim containment of such a protuberance is providing intolerable to say the least. You reach down and free the beast from its enclosure; ah, that's better.

After a while you get your sea legs and hobble into the kitchen. You polish off a litre of fresh orange juice in an attempt to quench your biblical thirst; rehydration being the name of the game. It brings about a partial resuscitation effect and you spot a note fixed to the fridge door with a novelty magnet, boldly addressed in Russell's hand to you. It goes along the lines of: thereafter you steadily deteriorated into a state of half-collapse; you ruined everybody's fucking evening you base cunt; but hey, hope you're feeling a bit better all the same. Rosalind, you're warned, is less forthcoming with regards to forgiveness and as far as your recovery goes, she couldn't care less one way of the other. You take that to mean you've blown your chance of ever spearing her bearded clam. C'est la fucking vie.

You start to remember stuff: their sleazy offer; The Borg; dancing in the street; how euphoric you initially felt when the Dove kicked in. You can safely say you're feeling the diametrical opposite of that today. Inside your head it's literally pandemonium; devilish fuckers have set up shop and are doling out retribution like there's no tomorrow. It feels like you're being trepanned from within, but then you're reminded of a sovereign remedy.

You enter that most private of domains; somebody else's

bedroom. This one looks just like any other, a bedroom is a bedroom, is a bedroom. But this one's Russell and Rosalind's and you haven't come in here to admire the natty décor or catch forty winks; you're here purely for fantasy and masturbatory purposes. You park yourself four-square on the bed and dick in hand, pants around ankles, set about achieving your objective. Whilst there are no personnel shortages in the Engorgement Dept., upstairs in Imagery most of the staff have rung in sick. An internal memo has been posted to your hippocampus: *'Due to reckless management improprieties, all higher mental activity has been suspended for the foreseeable future. Apologies for any inconvenience caused.'* Now you need to find an alternative method of stimulation to support the matter in hand: visual, aural, or…olfactory. At the foot of the bed, like a pot of gold at the end of a rainbow, lie Rosalind's strewn and obviously well worn panties. The role of knicker-sniffer is not a part you ever saw yourself auditioning for, but you've always said you shouldn't knock anything till you've tried it, so in for a penny…

Once you've got Rosalind's smalls over your head and positioned accordingly, you take your partner by the hand and dance a vigorous five-knuckle shuffle. Minutes pass; you find yourself consumed by that most characteristic of designer fragrances: *Parfum du Rosalind*. In fact what you've fashioned for yourself here is a relative *bouquet garni*, and it's enhanced this ordinary meat dish to almost *haute cuisine* specifications. Languidly, incautiously, you continue to pull the head off.

In no time at all, you're galloping down the home straight with only a furlong to go, when you're suddenly aware of an unannounced human presence in the room. You pull aside your insanitary blindfold and find its gob smacked owner standing there, bracing herself in the doorway. Not only have you been caught with your pants down in the true meaning of the phrase, you've been undeniably exposed with her pants *on*.

No verbal communication is forthcoming and you offer her none in return. The room is filled with a short-lived tranquillity and for one merciful instant, you think she might just see the funny side. But that old proverb about women scorned: you wonder whether its author was ever bubbled in a similarly compromising configuration as the one you now find yourself to be in. By such things does fate do its work for you conclude as her fists windmill into your cowering aberration of a body.

Expectanz
Jane Graham

When we come in from sitting out in the yard I see that he has taken up gymnastics in the meantime. With hands and feet splayed out to the sides he jumps up and down in the shape of a star until he has had enough and then stands, waiting, tapping his foot restlessly on the floor of the cavern as if to say, so kids, when are we going to get this show back on the road?

Our miniature warrior sits inside the television screen, all set to go now that his magical abilities have recharged and his health is back at its peak. He seems oblivious to the fact he's stood smack bang in the middle of a blazing furnace being tended to by a gang of ogres chiselled wholly out of rocks, apparently as immersed in their activity as he is in his. Just as soon as one of us restarts the game though, they'll notice him and attack.

Just then, the baby kicks. It doesn't mess about, this one, in handing out the hidings, and when I pull up my top we can both see the distinct imprint of a foot bulging out of the stretched flesh of my stomach, as if this kid is trying to make a break for the outside world feet first.

Just two weeks now to go. That's if we're still running to schedule, of course. Lee thinks this one is going to be an early bird. I've had to hear him explain to me I don't know how many times how all the women in his family have their babies before the due date, but I'm not so sure. I don't wonder if it'll wait until August, just to let me sit out this long hot summer with my own built-in radiator.

I can't remember the last time we got this lucky with our seasons, when the weather's so fine you don't even have to bring a jacket in case, when you just know tomorrow's going to sweat the life out of you the same as today. Bloody typical the one June I'm under house arrest has to be heading for the hottest British summer in years. It reminds me of the ones when I was a kid, with hikes bilberry-picking on the moors; one year a patch of heather caught fire just like that in front of me and my brother, and us kneeling on the moorland with our gobs open looking at each other like, we didn't do nowt, honest, we didn't touch it! My mum always used to tell me it was like this when I was born.

I can still feel the heat coming up from the melting concrete out in the yard. That's more Lee's domain than mine. He's been smoking out there now that he doesn't freeze his nuts off soon as he opens the door – we both agree it's better for the baby that way - and he seems to know exactly what's going on with most of the neighbours, though to be honest that's one scenario I can live without exploring. The other day he started telling me about the group of students who live in the next house along. They keep their door open well into the evenings just like we do, and aside from their regular viewings of *Eastenders* they sound like they've got a right little soap opera going of their own. I wasn't too impressed when he said he kept seeing one of the girls in just her bra and knickers all the time, some little madam of a magistrate's daughter, necking bottles of vodka in her room half-naked. Took it with a pinch of salt though. In your dreams, I told him, trying to look pissy but he could see the dimples where the smile was coming through. All that was before we started the game, of course.

Just press the x key to pause it, Lee always has to tell me every time like it's the first. You would have thought I'd remember it by now but somehow I don't. It's the same key to start it up again, I do know that much. Even when you've paused it, though, the game figure doesn't stop going through the motions, but it's a computer-generated loop, that's all, just a series of actions repeated over and over until play is resumed or the machine is turned off completely.

Lee starts the game up once more but he's not concentrating properly and three ogres ambush him all at once. I'm dead, he says, emitting just a moment's tantrum of body language and then he's starting it again from his last save point like nothing happened.

That's Lee, tenacious as a terrier with a postman's ankle. He'll play for hours without tiring. The father of my unborn child, lying on his stomach and propped-up on his elbows, the sun dappling his body in stripes of light through the slatted blinds in a profile of complete concentration, his mouth a little open and his brow furrowed. I suppose he might quit if I suddenly jumped up off the bed, a great wet patch where I'd been sitting, but I doubt there's much else to distract us this week. We'll just keep playing until lumpy here decides it's time.

It might not seem like it as I never go near the controls, but I assure you we play this game together. I'm more of a back-seat driver, letting Lee know when he needs to use a healing potion or a magic spell, warning him of things he can't see he's so caught up in the fighting, trying to figure out the puzzles and how all the gems work. Hand me the joystick, and I'll be dead within a minute, and that only makes me cranky and short-tempered. This way works out fine.

I do take breaks away from it sometimes to have a nap or a walk to the supermarket, let Lee carry on without me. The first game we played together I didn't take my eyes off the television screen for hours at a time, and then there I was in the night, talking about dragons and magic rings in my sleep. Now the baby keeps me grounded, I suppose. Always needing to get up to take a pee, to eat, always that restless fidgeting just in case I might forget I was really pregnant.

If the last eight months have seen me bloom I must be the Venus Fly Trap of expectant mothers. Fierce close combat and an aggression rating at times off the chart don't seem to have done too much harm, I mean I had wanted to get a whole new set of cups in the kitchen anyway. Most of the time money was at the bottom of it all, but all sorts of shit have prompted me to lose it since Christmas. Protecting my ward, call it what you like – just lately, though, we seem to have found ourselves becalmed, like being tossed up after a storm in the Bermuda Triangle.

At least physically, I seem to have taken to pregnancy like a duck to water, and as for the two of us, we've slid into a little routine of our own, one based around that machine. It starts too early for the jobless, granted, as the morning sun has become an impatient authority that we try in vain to escape, crawling into the quilt for peaceful darkness, sheets sticking to our sweaty bodies. Yet aside from this capitulation to the weather and with a break for an afternoon siesta, our days are spent in the game.

I'd made him put it away. It's not good for us, I'd said, it's rotting our brains. Stopping me sleeping and learning all those lines, which is what I was supposed to be doing back then. I was determined to get my big break. I needed to rehearse, audition, hell, do something. Even when I found out I was pregnant, in the beginning that only seemed to make it worse. Barely a few more months of my life as I knew it left to cram in everything I hadn't got around to before… Who was I kidding? I got bored and asked him to get it out of the box again.

The Playstation, I mean. Can we play it, I'd say, meaning I wanted him to play it and for me to watch. This really annoys Lee sometimes. He gets tired of my constant commentary, do this,

208

watch out for that, tells me I have no idea how difficult it actually is to fight the enemies with this joystick. I know I might make it look easy, he says… That's Lee for you, not exactly weighed down with humility.

I don't want to go out. I have everything I need right here. I don't need start doing things out there when I don't know when I'll have to down tools and leg it for the hospital. It's okay just to watch Lee make his way through the caverns.

They call this 'nesting', don't they? Except I'm supposed to be decorating our spare room with balloon-motifed wallpaper and fuzzy sky blue/pink things until it's sickly enough to be dubbed 'the nursery', if we had a spare room, that is. We just have a cot, and Lee's already put that together. Took him about half-an-hour. Now if I'd have tried to assemble it, I could have probably killed a couple of days.

Lee's getting agitated with this particular part of the game. He makes me go and look at a walk-through on the computer. I call up the file in documents and scroll through it until I find the tips for this level, but they're not exactly useful. It was probably written by some spotty Japanese twelve year old; surely nobody could stand to be the wife or the girlfriend of someone whose entire free time was spent on the computer systematically noting every enemy, object - magic or otherwise - and puzzle encountered in this entire adventure game.

Lee's not impressed with the information I give him but it's not my fault the spotty Japanese kid didn't think the level worthy of closer attention.

People keep telling me I won't be able to be like this after the baby is born, like I didn't know that. My mum gave me a book to read but all I've done with that is laugh at the pictures. I don't suppose I'll really be missing much if this is what I'm giving up. I'm sure I did once have more than days like today, but what, I couldn't quite tell you – more nights than days, for one thing. I've tracked the loss of my figure by the week, but my memory ran away when my back was turned.

Before I can sink back into the mattress and lose myself in the game, I decide we need tea, so I take the used cups from off the side into the kitchen with me, trying to make sure I don't make too much noise. Pregnancy has made me very heavy-footed, and Lee is always berating me for stomping, which would mean that I was stroppy about something, and isn't usually the case. I just walk like that now without thinking, though I still don't reckon Lee believes me. I put the kettle on, then notice there's no milk. We live round the back of a shop, one owned by the landlord, so it's no big deal to go out and get some. If I ever forget that fact, there's little things to remind me, like when they've just had a delivery and you can hear them, lugging great sacks of onions or potatoes or whatever it is down into the cellar. I guess they can hear us just as well in the shop, too.

Out in the yard the sun shoots me a glare of such vehemence that I squint my eyes in half-blindness, my vision returning just in time to see next-door's cat mid-dump and intent on burying her shit by the side of the drainage hole. Ever since the woman on the corner kicked her out of that square foot of rose garden for making too many holes she's had this vain hope that one day she'll be able to dig her way through concrete.

I don't walk like some pregnant women, like they're dragging a cement mixer around with them; I give my step a bit of a bounce but it's an odd kind of gait, what with my shoulders pushed back and my spine a little arched, which I read somewhere is the worst thing you can do, and will probably lead to backache. If it starts hurting me I'll stop doing it, but by this point it's grown into kind of a habit. Now that my stomach has swelled I feel much more comfortable, that everything is how it should be, very public and on display. I can see the people sat drinking outside the pub on the other side of the road, partaking in a nice pint or two on a hot summer afternoon. One of them looks over, probably notices some lass got herself knocked-up. I don't mind; I feel validated by my size. For months all I've had to put up with is 'But, you're so thin' remarks probably meant as compliments but which succeeded in making me feel like a fraud. At least now I know I haven't imagined the whole thing.

The only person who seemed to notice in the beginning was the woman at the bakery where I used to go every weekday morning on my way to work to buy a cake. 'D'you know yet if it's a girl or a boy?' the middle-aged woman had asked me one day when I was about four or five months pregnant. I'd looked down at my stomach and the woman had nodded, patted her own belly and smiled. It was winter then, and I'd always been dressed in a thick coat and sweater every time I went in there, and I was so thin even the midwife was starting to wonder when I was going to expand. How could the woman have known? 'Of course I can tell, it's one of those things women just know,' the baker had responded cryptically, adding a beatific smile.

The old Pakistani women from one of the other houses that share our yard are creeping slowly along the concrete, a pair of wrapped objects, their bodies two amorphic shrouds of loose cotton, barely moving, like enormous snails in front of me. They take up most of the space, and I have to remind myself that I can no longer slither through the gap in the way that I used to. I always miscalculate the area needed for the addition of the bump. I gad slowly to the rear, watching my sandalled feet rise and then fall.

I'm bringing in the tea I've finally finished making through from the kitchen, which is like five steps, along with some biscuits I found on top of the fridge I'd forgotten about, surmising that it's a nice change from looking for things I've already eaten, when I have one of those hormonal waves of sentiment. I lean against the wall with my legs out straight and long and stare straight ahead of me for a couple of moments. I like our house, I say to Lee all of a sudden, I wish we didn't have to move.

But we do have to move, in three months. It's hard to know if we should start looking before or after the baby is born. Before might be too soon, but after might be too difficult. After, how can I even picture afterwards, if I don't know where it will be set?

The thing about this house, even if it hasn't got a spare room, is that we have this huge living room that we're in now. Only suddenly I can't help noticing that it doesn't seem so vast and spacious anymore, what with that cot swallowing up so much of my glorious space.

I got so panicked about having the baby early I decided we had to go out and buy a cot, which of course came flat-packed but Lee being like every male I've ever met had to put it up the very same afternoon when we got it and now it sits there, collecting dust bunnies underneath it so that we can hang our clothes over the bars instead of our usual habit of discarding them on the floor. We should probably get out of the habit of doing that before the baby starts sleeping in it. I never expected it to be so bulky, to take up quite so much of the room. I guess when I pictured it in my mind I was imagining one of those cribs, those dainty artefacts like painted eggs always swaying so sweetly in the shop windows but which are basically pointless purchases given that the baby will have grown out of it within four or five months. But this is a full-size cot, all right.

I remember when we bought it, how they were in the shop. This woman, miserable as sin she was. I always thought you had to be permanently full of the joys of spring to work in somewhere like Mothercare, all smiles and congratulations and bliss at being the ones to provide for our little miracles. But we had some YTSer who just wanted to file her nails and *wont right sure*. At the time I only asked if they had one in stock, and she said she'd have to check, but when we heard a great clunking and scraping of cardboard packaging being lugged back up the stairs Lee turned to me and said, Oh God, we'd better have it now, we can't ask her to take it back down there again.

Lee's not from these parts, a London boy he is and can't understand how people round here can be so miserable. I keep telling him, we're not really so depressed as you make out, it just seems that way, I allow him that, and maybe we're not into forcing a happy demeanour in everyone's faces whether they like it or not. You know how they are down in London, my uncle used to say, all smarmy and smiles, like they want something out of you. All false. All two-faced. Lee thinks we're nuts.

I know the cot's only the beginning. The baby stuff is coming, encroaching steadily across the room until there's just us, and the sofa-bed, the television and the Playstation in this corner.

I look over at Lee. He doesn't notice I'm staring at him; I think he must still be in the computer game, in his head, off killing ogres and witches, considering his tactics for getting through the rest of this level, trying to predict what he's about to come up against.

I'll admit I'm not quite with it myself. Funny how a thought as innocent as having to stop leaving my cardigan in the cot once the baby is born could lead to such a panic in my mind. I can't get past the maternity ward. If we can't get this warrior through this cavern region, how can I get myself past the childbirth?

Maybe it's just that I've got too much time on my hands. I

figured at one point I needed to take some time to meditate on my condition; hippy bollocks probably, but anyway. I didn't even bother trying to explain how I felt to Lee, 'cause he's already of the opinion that I think more than is healthy. I finished work too early, really, but it's hard to clean offices without being able to bend down and get back up again quickly and easily. They took me off the most strenuous tasks, but that didn't leave all that much for me to do. My boss told me to stay on for longer, no use sitting at home and brooding, she said, keep yourself busy, I worked right up until the week before I had my first one, no problem at all. I guess our generation lack the work ethic of our elders; I could hardly wait for an excuse to leave.

As for Lee, he has still got a job, not that you'd know it of late. He hasn't taken any shifts in the nightclub that hired him for almost a month now. He has this paranoia the baby will come in the middle of a shift, and nobody will hear the phone over the din when I try to call. Like I said, he's convinced this one's impatient to get out.

Sometimes I feel like I should be doing something else and I wish he was at work and then I try to make a list of the things I still need to buy, but I always get bored with that in about five minutes and find myself eager to get back to the game, where everything is understandable and straightforward, the ending is clear and tasks are prescribed. Maybe if Lee was at work I would be finding myself cleaning out the kitchen cupboards instead.

How many levels are there to this, anyway? I ask Lee but he doesn't answer, he's in the middle of some bloody combat and I don't think I should have disturbed him with a question. I wonder if we'll finish it before the baby is born. And if that happens, I can't think how we're going to pass the time while we're waiting.

Crime Class

Mark Costello

Morning...

If you have a certificate that claims you are a teacher, does that mean you can educate, instruct and teach? And even if you can, surely by virtue of you wanting to be a teacher suggests you are brainless and therefore not a responsible person to instil ideas in others, especially when your own ideas are preoccupied with the imaginings of vicarious mischief; violence and death, or the romance of alcoholic French sailors pissing on cobblestones. For my sins I am now cast as a teacher. My first day as a teacher was a tragedy, I am now at the point of farce readying myself for a new class in the world of further education. On mornings like this I think 'He who can, does. He who cannot, is a cunt, also known as a teacher.'

Are my eyes really brown? What would the reader like to know about me? I was born when man first landed on the moon. I am thirty-five, live alone and am too embarrassed to use the smaller 'bachelor' trolleys in supermarkets. I feel a mixture of pity and contempt for those who buy the little half-tins of beans. I pity their solitude and am contemptuous of their inability to eat a full tin like a proper person. I have worked in a Further Education College for five years. Work is a pain and fills me with distaste. Other teachers annoy me. They seem interested in what they are doing and appear to believe it is worthy. If emptying dustbins were better paid, that would be my preferred occupation. It is an important social function and this disposable society would be totally fucked and more full of shit if it didn't exist. Can the same be said for further education?

I am worried about my weight at the moment. I always used to look at my dad's fat gut and think, that's not going to be me. But it is. People remark on how much I look like my dad even down to the increased waistband. Where did all this weight come from? I used to be slim, energetic, attractive to the opposite sex, and now, well, I'm not like that anymore. I've had to admit defeat and move from medium straight to extra large. I could use my position I suppose to entice some woman. The intellectual attraction, positive strokes of the modern, sensitive, thinking man. Ah but I can't be bothered. The energy levels have plummeted. I've become a ritualist, dragging myself through life and work; my only solace, the bottle and music, oh and an unhealthy interest in documentaries about Nazis.

I always get a bit worried on the morning of a new class. Anxieties trouble me. Have I prepared enough? How will it go? Most of the teachers who have taught me in Further Education, Adult Education, University, training or whatever have been generally poor really. Well, not poor more uninspiring. I want to be inspiring, can I stress that, I'd love to be inspiring, for people to leave thinking that was good. But that's the real problem, I think I'm actually very boring. I try and think who I can gain inspiration from myself to become more than I am. On the beginning of *Don't Let Me Down* by the Beatles, John Lennon urges the others to play loud and 'give me the courage to come screaming in…' That's what we all need, the courage to come screaming in.

So OK I've got a class this morning, the first of ten weekly two-hour sessions, An Introduction to Criminology, the crime class.

Starting…

My dad who has done his fair share of courses at college, used to always get stopped by new students who thought he was one of the teachers. With me, the opposite is true. The crime class is taking place in a community centre away from college. This pleases me. It's timetabled for Friday mornings 9.30–12.30, this also pleases me. It means there's the potential to slope off after and go to the pub instead of going back to work. This thought pleases me the most.

I go into the building, set up the room and get my stuff out. Soon after, the first student comes in.

'Are you here for the crime class?' she asks.

'Yes.' I answer.

'I hope it's good,' she said. 'last time I came on a course run by this college it was useless.'

I smile. Great, I think. A picky learner, actually wants something interesting. 'Well I'll do my best. My name's Charlie by the way, I'm the teacher.'

'Oh sorry,' she said. 'I'm Tracy, I thought you were a student.'

'I'll take that as a compliment Tracy. Would you like a cup of tea or coffee?'

I took the order and vanished to the kitchen to put the kettle on. When I returned with Tracy's drink there were another half-dozen or so folk in the room. I said hello, told them we'd do the introductions in a minute or two. We waited a few moments more and another one rolled in. I checked their names on my list, full house. When I'd made sure that everyone had a drink, I vanished again, this time to the toilet, where I punched the air and snorted like Robert De Niro as Jake La Motta in *Raging Bull*. 'C'mon, c'mon, c'mon, c'mon', I repeated, my mantra for the morning, 'you can do it, you can do it, you can do it, you can do it.' Someone came out of one of the toilets. It was the centre caretaker.

'Alright?' I enquired.

'Are you having trouble shitting mate?' he asked, 'I've got some suppositories in me cloister.'

Back in the class, the students are seated in anticipatory fashion, eyes pointing in my direction.

'OK folks, just before we get going, we'll get the enrolment forms out of the way.' That one always kills a bit of time. Nullifies any potentially positive vibes and takes away the edge of excitement, the negation.

That over, I ask for them to introduce themselves and why they are here today. In no particular order their names are Andrew, Dave, Barbara, Karen, Anne, Donna, Paul and Tracy. They work in or represent, again in no particular order, the prison service, a young person's unit, a psychiatric institution, court official, ex P.A. drug and alcohol service. In other words, a right bunch. Most agreed that the main reason they were here was to understand what motivates people to be criminals especially those who kill, torture and mutilate. I have a suspicion that the prison officers are on a bit of a skive, but I don't mind that, so am I. I say something about myself, not quite on the lines of I'm a fat, boring turd although that's what I'm thinking. I take a moment. I mustn't let it slip. I take hold of a quick vision of Richard Harris in *Cromwell*, before asking:

'What is crime?'

Donna is the first to answer.

'It's doing wrong' she says. Donna's about my age. Actually she's a couple of years older. I note on her enrolment form her age and that she's married. A shame, she's not bad looking. Nicely put together. I compose my thoughts.

'Yes it could be doing wrong,' I say. 'But do we all agree what is right and wrong. Do you think for instance that drinking is wrong?'

'It couldn't be more right,' laughs Dave. I like his tone. He's in his forties, a wiry thing, with a short crop and goatee. He's one of the prison officers, one of the lads. I hope he has no self-control when it comes to drinking, I hope he doesn't know when to stop.

'Drinking is socially acceptable in this country, but in others it isn't. In fact you can be severely punished for drinking alcohol in some countries,' I say. 'So is crime…' I pause for effect…'a matter of right and wrong?'

'But surely there are some things that are just wrong aren't there? Like killing,' says Anne, the sixty-odd year-old ex-Personal Assistant. Paul takes up the challenge. Another thin one, how do these people stay so thin, don't they eat? I know, I know, it's their metabolism. God I should know I'll be teaching about the theory of Somatotypes later.

'What about war? Doesn't that involve killing?' he says.

'Yes, but that's different surely?' answers Anne.

'Different?' I ask. 'What makes one act of killing right and another wrong?' There's a moment's silence, before Tracy announces that it's to do with the law.

'That's right,' I say. 'What is crime? It is any action that breaks the legally defined rules of a society. It's as simple as that.' But is it as simple as that? I suggest that it is further complicated by our own individual beliefs and morals. 'There may be many things that are against the law that we can be punished for, but should we? Conversely there are ways of behaving that many people may find offensive, but are not legally punishable.'

'How do you mean?' says Andrew, a rotund, grinning baldie.

'What I am talking about here is deviance, meaning to move from the norm.' They look puzzled. 'We all accept that there are certain ways of behaving, right? Waiting our turn, not jumping queues, being reasonable. But then we see others doing things out of the ordinary, things that are not the norm. It could be as simple as someone talking very loudly in public places, men wearing women's clothes, especially in public. Anything that the majority of people would consider unusual or unacceptable behaviour.'

'So presumably sexuality can come into this,' says Tracy.

'Of course,' I say. 'And a moral dimension comes into this as well. A lot of religious institutions view homosexuality as amoral, and some individuals see it as abnormal.'

'And it used to be illegal,' says Tracy.

'That's right,' I agreed, 'and in the past, even enlightened scientists saw it as a disease that could be cured, or a mental aberration. So. There is crime and there is deviance. There are law-breakers and norm-breakers. Not all criminals are necessarily deviants, and not all deviants are criminals. Why? Because no matter what people think, I can't be locked up for wearing my mother's old dresses, sitting in a rocking chair and watching *Psycho* all day. Similarly someone can be locked up for protesting against an unpopular measure. Would we see this person as a deviant? Perhaps not.'

I'm pleased with the way we've started. I decide to keep up the momentum by getting them all to do a crime survey. It involves a series of questions, such as *Have you ever driven over 30mph in a 30mph speed limit area? Have you ever used your work phone for personal calls? Have you ever taken stationary from work?* Of course most have done one thing or another, and since most of the things on the list carry a maximum six months prison sentence for theft or fraud, or a £5000 fine, cumulatively one or two of them are looking at a prison stretch of a couple of years or more or heavy fines.

'I get it,' says Andrew. 'We're all criminals, right.'

I smile.

'Well I knew that anyway about myself,' he continues, 'I spent six months in the nick as a kid, but I never went back.'

'That must mean you're either a reformed character,' I say. 'Or else you're a better criminal than you used to be.'

'Neither,' Andrew retorts, 'just a sad, old bastard. Excuse the French.'

'You don't look that old,' says Tracy.

'We can't comment on the sad bastard bit,' joins in Dave, laughing.

'But you wouldn't get in trouble for these things would you?' asks Karen, the other prison officer. She's a big woman, very imposing and she looks you right in the eye when speaking. I've noticed Paul eyeing her up already and we've only been here half-an-hour.

'Well you know, you're right. It usually only happens in extreme cases,' I say. 'There were a couple of blokes at a local tyre manufacturer that were ripping off tyres for months before they got caught. They should have stopped, but they got greedy and the company were on to it. But anything taken from work is theft, and it gives some employers the opportunity to get rid of employees if they want to. I can imagine some unscrupulous firm wanting to get rid of staff, but not wanting to pay out redundancies and using theft of company property as an excuse.'

I've got them, they're all nodding their heads, pondering. Donna's impressed I can see. Her eyes are on me. I need to think of something erudite to say now.

'As Aristotle once said *The roots of education are bitter, but the fruit is sweet*. And if you believe that,' I say, 'you'll believe anything. We've shown that we've all broken the law, but we don't regard this as deviant behaviour. Thus as I said before, you can quite easily be a criminal, but not a deviant.'

At break time I have a chat to Barbara. She works in the Magistrates court, showing people around. But I think she'd really like to live in the Crown court, she seems to spend most of her spare time there at any rate. She's a latter-day Madame Lafarge.

'Ooh I've seen some trials in my time,' she says, 'but my greatest regret is not being able to see the Yorkshire Ripper.'

'Oh yes, I can understand that.' I say. Though I tell her not to worry, there might be another serial killer coming up in the future that she get can get tickets for.

'If I'm lucky,' she says. Paul chips in. He's wandered over from the other side of the room, spilling half of his tea on the way.

'But what about all the poor buggers that'll have to die for you to see some Court action?' he says.

'There's always a downside to everything,' answers Barbara.

'Any views on how they should go?' adds Andrew.

'I'd favour garrotting,' says Paul. 'Bring back Fu Man Chu.'

'Alright gang, let's get back to it,' I say.

I'm feeling quite powerful now, the warm-up in the toilet must have worked. The mantra is seeing me through. It's time to move on to the next level – think Peter O' Toole in *Lawrence of Arabia* decked out in white with the golden desert and blue skies behind him. A powerful thought. Wait a minute though, now I'm thinking of him being molested by José Ferrer.

'Right everyone,' I say banishing the thought from my head, 'a little exercise, I want you to name three criminals that you admire and a couple that you don't.'

'I can't think of any,' says Andrew. The rest of the group set to it and come up with an assortment of gangsters, except Tracy who has named Muhammad Ali. Interesting choice I tell her.

'Yes, he was cast as a criminal for refusing the draft and not going to fight in the Vietnam war,' I say. 'Villain or hero, it's not clear cut is it?'

Criminals that the group didn't admire came more easily, Hitler, the Moors Murderers, Dennis Nilson, Peter Sutcliffe, Harold Shipman and other mass murderers, serial killers and assorted nutters.

'Will we be doing about serial killers?' asks Donna. I don't want to disappoint her. Between two buttons of her blouse I can just see her bra and a bit of flesh. Christ I'm a right perv.

'Yes, we'll certainly touch on it,' I say. 'Actually before we move on, let me ask you all some questions. See if this describes you.' I nod and wink in Donna's direction.

'Are you a compulsive masturbator?' I don't stop for the sniggers. 'Are you a chronic liar? Do you wet the bed? Are you rebellious? Do you suffer from nightmares? Do you like setting fire to things? Do you have a poor body image? Do you have temper tantrums? Do you have sleep problems? Do you have phobias? Are you cruel to animals? Have you got an eating disorder? Do you daydream?'

'That sounds like me,' says Andrew.

'Quick everybody, I say, 'get out of the room now, come on, we have a serial killer in our midst.' This time I do stop for laughter, but there isn't any. 'No, this information has been taken from a study involving a number of imprisoned serial killers in America. It actually charts the childhood behaviour traits amongst serial killers. Anyway it leads us on to the next question Are criminals born or made? Have a think about it for a couple of minutes and discuss it in pairs.'

They're chatting away, that's good, gives me a bit of time to think what to say next. It's a painful process for me. I really need some help to plan more effectively. When I was in training, another student and I were asked to cover a class at the last minute. The proper teacher had just phoned in sick. We were both panicking, but his was outward and mine inward. I just got on with it.

Afterwards he said, I wish I had your ability to be spontaneous. I said, the problem is I'm only spontaneous because I'm so shit at planning, I have to do things on the spot because I only ever have a basic grasp of what I'm going to do beforehand, and it's frightening at times.

'Some people are just born bad,' says Barbara. 'They're evil.'

'Others might become criminal out of circumstance,' adds Tracy. 'It could be through poverty or whatever.'

'Right' I say, 'what we have looked at today is the act of crime and that of deviance. Crime is not set in stone. One person can kill multiple victims and be locked up for the rest of their life, another can kill many more and be lauded as a great soldier or flying ace. Some things in the past which were criminal are no longer so, such as homosexuality or having abortions. There are other things that have become illegal but were not in the past, such as the use of drugs particularly of the class A variety. Remember Sherlock Holmes and his seven per cent solution. Having sexual relations with girls as young as twelve would be seen as abuse today, but would have been quite normal in the past. Regular acts of discrimination towards different ethnic groups and women were perfectly acceptable before the late sixties and early seventies. Racial Discrimination and Equal Opportunities/Equal Pay Acts made those practices illegal. How we identify criminals changes over time and from place to place. Can we therefore say that criminals are born or have some genetic quality that marks them out as law-breakers?'

'It does become a little less straightforward,' says Anne. 'But surely the likes of Hitler, dictators are evil and born that way?'

'Hitler perpetrated a holocaust against a nation of people,' I say, 'but he is not alone in this. In both the ancient and modern world, many civilizations have been wiped out by conquering or ruling forces; the Carthaginians by Rome, the Aztecs by the Spanish, the Native Americans by the United States. Tens of millions of Africans were enslaved by the British and Americans, many of these were killed or died in transit across the Atlantic or on American plantations. Aborigines and Maoris in Australia and New Zealand have suffered at the hands of new occupiers. Stalin killed millions of Russians in purges, human decimation has occurred in Kampuchea, Rwanda and countless other places. Mass murder has been a constant in the nineteenth and twentieth centuries. Are those responsible for all these things evil, or is it the nature of the world they live in, one of violent domination and subjugation?'

When the world is an insane place, show me the benefits of sanity, I think.

'So,' says Andrew, 'you're saying criminals are made?'

'Well I would say that criminals are made by their own society's definition of what constitutes law-breaking. And there we have to leave it.'

Time's up. I finish by telling them that we will be starting to look at some explanations next week, and the origins of criminology.

They look pleased enough as they leave. Of course the big test is whether they come back again next week.

Afternoon…

I decide to go for a quick drink. There's a new pub recently opened down the road and it's selling cheap beer at the moment. When I get inside, I see Paul at the bar, he's just getting one in.

'How do?' he says.

'Not bad,' I say. 'What you supping?'

'John Smith's,' he says.

'Is it alright?' I say.

'Aye, not bad.' he ask.

'Good, I'll have one,' I say. Jesus Christ the art of conversation is far from dead.

'Have you been in here before?' I ask.

'Aye,' he says. 'There's a stripper on on Thursdays, I came in to watch her shake her tits.'

Thursdays, I thought. I'll have to make a mental note of that. I could be passing and call in on Thursday. If anyone sees me I can say, I don't believe this, I've just come out for a quiet pint and I'm faced with this. It's disgusting, it's degrading to womanhood. Yes very…

I get Paul one in. He gets me one back, then I get off. I'm on the bus home, but I'm bursting for the bog. I know I'll never make it home, so I nip in the local to use the facilities. Whilst I'm there, I get a drink in. I say it's my local, in the sense that it's the closest pub to my home, but it's not a place you'd find me very often. Anyway I'm in there a few hours and I've seen it go from empty to full, from the old brigade having a drink before they go home for their tea and telly to youngsters having one on their way out for the night. Here I am, neither young nor old, slowly getting pissed before going home to face a pot noodle – great. I wonder what Donna's up to? I wonder if I should get a few cans from the shop and a dirty mag to have a wank over? I check my pockets and upon finding only £2, decide to have one more drink here then bugger off.

A Dog in a Bag
Michael Stewart

— Hi, how was work? Liz was looking at the TV as she spoke.

— OK. There was a man with a dog in a bag on the bus this morning.

— Really. Her eyes still aligned with the set. Andrew threw his coat into the corner of the room and closed the door behind him.

— Sshh! She pointed to the baby-chair where their daughter was sleeping.

— Sorry. Has she been asleep long?

— She's been skriking for over an hour, she's just gone off.

He loosened his tie and continued with the day's itinerary unprompted. — Then, when I got off and walked up Church Street, a van stopped at the crossing. An old green van. A man was driving it, an old grey man. And sat next to him, you'll never guess what.... She didn't respond, her eyes were directed towards the TV as before.

— ...A woman. In a pink dress and jet black hair. Only it wasn't. It was a mannequin. It was a mannequin sat next to the man not a woman, and he'd dressed it up in a fifties outfit.

— Really. She did not look away from the screen.

He came and sat down next to her. — What are you watching?

— Jerry. She moved some magazines and papers to make room for him, placing them on the coffee table automatically.

— What's it about?

She looked over at him for the first time. Their eyes didn't meet as he was now watching the TV.

231

— It's about couples who have no time for sex. They're wanting to spice up their sex lives, so they've made these home videos.

There were two couples sat in a television studio on a podium in front of a studio audience. Dennis and Jackie, the couple on the right, were talking about a film they had made with Jackie dressed as a French maid. A short extract is played with Dennis on a hotel bed being attended to by Jackie in a skimpy maid outfit. As she bends over her red silk knickers are visible. He slaps her behind. She squeals. Jerry then introduces us to Richard and Charlene, who are sat to the left and have been enacting a film script of Tarzan. We are once again shown an extract. Charlene is bikinied and rubbing oil on the exposed part of her chest. Richard is gyrating in a leopard skin loin cloth to the sound of 'Wim Away' by Tight Fit. Jerry now asks for volunteers from the audience to go to a hotel and film themselves having sex.

What Jerry wants to know, is whether this couple from the audience will do things on film that they wouldn't do ordinarily. We'll find out after the commercial break.

He picked up a paper from the coffee table and turned to the classified column. He mulled over the adverts, before reading out loud, — box files, twelve, 50p each…Why would anyone advertise that?

No response.

— How about this: four thousand boot and shoe laces, assorted colours, £300… He turned the page. — Hey, this sounds good: two first-class return tickets with Delta airlines, to any destination in the world, from any UK airport where Delta fly…£120.

She nodded blankly.

He skimmed the rest of the column. — Aggressive roller blades? Leslie speaker? Ransom potato spinner? Balk tank? Still no response. — I haven't got a clue what any of this stuff is, have you?

The show was starting again. He lowered the paper, half-watching, half scanning the classified columns.

— Hi, welcome back.

Jerry recapitulates. He asks the question he left the viewers with at the end of the first half, this time to the couple from the audience who are now seated in the centre of the podium, with Dennis and Jackie to their left and Richard and Charlene to their right. They are called Marvin and Sandy.

Marvin: — It makes it more better.

Sandy: — You know why? He directed the whole time, he told me what to do, where to go, everything.

This gets a laugh from the audience. Of course there's a point to all this: 'Video Sex – How to Transform Your Sex Lives' by Dr Andy Peterson. Marvin sums up the profound benefits of this to the audience: — Ahr think you folks should awl go buy this video… Shee worz dooin' thangs ahr never seen done before… The audience clap and cheer in approval.

It's back to Jerry for the final thought: — Lights, camera, action! You may not win an Oscar but you might win a spouse. It's two thumbs up for Dr Peterson, and heaven knows what else!

Andrew went back to reading the classifieds. — Terran trade authority handbooks, full set required, will pay up to £30 if in good condition…What the hell are Terran trade authority handbooks?

She turned to him, suddenly remembering. — Hey, guess what I discovered today?

He looked up from his paper. — Eh?

— This thing…She took hold of the baby intercom. — It picks up next door.

He put the paper down. — How do you mean?

— Well, they've had a baby girl too, haven't they, a few weeks after us. They must have one of these as well. They're really sensitive, you can hear every word over it. There's two channels see. She showed him the switch underneath which determined the channel.

— How do you know?

— She had a sleep this afternoon, so I had it turned on, and I must have had it on the wrong channel. At first I could just hear her breathing. But then she woke up and started crying, and I thought, that's not our baby. It was a different sound, more high-pitched. I was just about to go into her room when I heard this voice, her voice next door, through the speaker, talking to her baby girl.

He smiled to himself. For some reason he found this amusing. But then, — Hang on, if we can hear them, then they must be able to hear us, right?

— Yeah, I know, I'll have to go round later and explain, make sure we use different channels.

She seemed disappointed at this. He stood up and went to the door. — Fancy a drink?

She shrugged. — What you making?

— Whatever.

— I'll have whatever you're having.

He began to open the door. She called him back as he was leaving the room. — What're you having?

— Probably a beer.

— I don't want a beer.

— Well what then?

— Something cold and long.

— I've got something hot and long… He winked at her.

— Don't be disgusting.

He left the room.

They ordered a couple of pizzas for tea, neither Andrew or Liz were in the mood for cooking. While they were waiting for them to be delivered, she went next door to have a word with Emily and Derek about the intercom. When she got back the pizzas had arrived and he handed her the hot box. She sat down beside him and they ate slices of soggy pizza as they stared at the Big Brother contestants on the telly.

— Well?

— Well what?

— Did you tell them?

She had told them and they had explained that, although they had an intercom, they didn't use it to listen to the baby, but instead as a night light, as it was a superior model to theirs and had this additional function. The baby was still in their room, see, so they didn't need it yet as an intercom. The receiver in Liz's intercom must be extremely sensitive to be able to pick up stuff, when they weren't even using it as an intercom, they all agreed. Liz told them that she wasn't able to hear anything properly, just that it lessened the reception. She agreed to use it only on a different channel, they seemed happy about this. She hadn't stayed long, but long enough to notice how nice they had got the place. She was telling Andrew this. He was listening as he chewed the mozzarella substitute cheese caught between his teeth.

— Well, they will have won't they, it's their own place.

Andrew and Liz rented the house they were living in. It was exactly the same as their next door neighbours' house in its design. But there was a lot of work needed doing on their house, while the Armours' house was fully modernised: central heating, double glazing, fitted kitchen, shower, loft insulation and at least three electrical sockets in each room. The Garrets' house, in contrast, was in dire need of a re-wire, a damp course, a change of window frames, a new door, both front and back, and new floors in the downstairs rooms.

Emily Armour had a reasonably well paid job as a team leader in a customer services department of an electrical supply company. Her boyfriend, Derek, worked in a bank in the centre of town. They each had their own cars. One was new, the other only a few years old. Andrew Garret worked for a telecommunications company. He'd been there several years, but had failed to get promoted, despite the fact that younger and less experienced staff had managed to rise above him in the ranks. Liz Garret worked as an auxiliary assistant in an old peoples' home. The pay was crap, but she didn't mind the job. She'd been there a few years now and felt settled. She didn't like change of any sort. It was out of the way. She sometimes worked odd hours and generally used the one car they owned, or rather would own next year when they had paid off the loan instalments.

Liz was already in bed when Andrew switched off the set for the night. He tidied up the living room, binning the cardboard boxes and empty beer tins, plumping up the cushions. The baby had been in bed for a few hours. They'd had a lot of sleepless nights at first but she generally slept through now. He unplugged the TV and went upstairs. Liz had left the bedroom light on, the frame of the door glowed orange at the end of the dark corridor. He pushed the door open very gently. She was still awake, sat up in bed with the intercom on her chest.

— What are you doing?

She looked over to him. — Come and have a listen to this.

— You're not listening to next door are you?

— It's weird, you can hear every sound…

He took his trousers off and draped them over the wardrobe door. — You shouldn't do, it's mean. How would you like it?

She looked indignant momentarily, then the guilt crept up. — I suppose you're right. She switched it back to the correct channel and placed it on the bedside cabinet. He climbed into bed beside her. He leant across and set the alarm for morning. He sat back in bed adjusting the pillows.

— What could you hear?

— Just the baby breathing at first but then I could hear them getting into bed. She was talking about going away for the weekend, her mum's looking after the baby for them. They've been invited to go on a TV programme. It's one of these talk shows, they wrote off for some free tickets last year and had forgotten about it, but they got a letter yesterday inviting them to come down and take part.

— And you heard all that? He cuddled up next to her, put his hand on her bare hip.

She recoiled. — Don't, your hands are freezing.

— I'll warm them up for you. He rubbed his hands together like a cartoon miser. His hands went beneath the sheets and made contact with her naked body once again. This time her recoil was more drastic, she seemed irritated.

— What have I told you, pack it in!

He sat upright and folded his arms.

— There's no need to shout. She didn't reply. She was curled up under the covers. The air was cold in the bedroom, despite the heater blowing out hot air. She pulled the sheets tightly around her, put her face beneath the duvet. He stared off into the distance, staring at the wall which separated their bedroom from the bedroom of Emily and Derek Armour. There was nothing on the wall, no pictures or posters, just a great expanse of magnolia covered wood chip. He leant across and took hold of the intercom. He flipped it over and switched it to the other channel. He turned up the volume and placed it to his ear.

Nothing. He could hear breathing, wasn't sure whose. Sounded like more than one person. He turned it up a bit more. Still nothing. He could now make out the stertorous respiration of the baby girl. Deep sleep. He could hear over this the sound of lighter, softer breath. It was somehow hypnotic. The sound of the night air being drawn in, warmed, and then released again. He could hear the bed squeak. He could hear two people kissing. The wet sound of their lips as they parted. He could hear the breath quicken and deepen. The bed began to groan rhythmically. He could hear now the distinct sound of someone panting. Another person groaning. The breath got faster still. The smack of the lips. Squelching. The bed's frantic protest. They were all groaning now, she, he, bed – in unison. Gasps of pleasure. Hot, urgent panting…

Liz grabbed the intercom from him and switched the channels. She put the unit back on the bedside cabinet.

— So it's OK for you to listen, but not me… Hypocrite! She disappeared under the covers again.

He jumped up and pulled the covers back, exposing her naked body to the cold air, her skin bristling, her nipples hardening. She stared at him aggressively. She looked down his body. He had an erection. He stared back at her. His look indecipherable. There was a long pause. Silence… Then the sound of their baby crying came through the speaker of the intercom. He got up and put his dressing gown on. She replaced the covers.

She listened to the intercom now. She heard, above the sound of her baby's cries, his steps on the corridor – at first fading, then getting louder. She heard the door of the baby's room open, and the floorboards creak as he approached the cot. She could hear his voice as he comforted his daughter. With the intercom's speaker held close it was like he was whispering in her ear and not the baby's.

— Hello baby, what you doing, what you doing little girl?

She could hear him lift her out of the cot.

— Is baby wet? Who's a wet little thing then…

She heard him open the changing box, take out a nappy and some baby wipes. She could hear the press studs pop open on the baby-grow. She had stopped crying now and was making soft gurgling noises. He was making raspberries on her naked body. His wet lips vibrating against her soft baby flesh. The baby giggled in excitement.

— You like that, don't you. Baby likes that, oh yes, oh yes… Want some more, baby want some more?

She wasn't tired anymore. She picked up the TV guide and skimmed through it. She flicked the switch on the remote and the television screen lit up the room, making it, somehow, feel warmer. She sat up and started to watch some late night talk show. It was put on at this time because it was supposed to be a bit risqué. He came back into the room. He looked at her then at the TV.

— Do you want a drink?

— What you making? She didn't look up at him, but at the TV screen.

— Whatever?

— I'll have whatever you're making.

He went out of the room, then popped his head round the door.

— I'm making something hot, do you want a cup of tea?

— No, I'll have a cold drink, in a big glass.

He closed the door without saying anything. Outside the

bedroom the house was as cold as the inside of a fridge. He switched the landing light on. His breath was smoke in front of his face. In the kitchen he heated the water in a pan. Their kettle had broke a few weeks ago. He'd have a flick through the classified column when he got back upstairs, see if he could find a second-hand one for sale. Money was tight. He glanced around the room. The walls were covered in green mould. A pool of water had formed behind the kitchen door. It was raining and there was a gap where the skirting had rotted. The water was boiling now and he made the tea. He took his mug and Liz's glass and went to switch off the light.

There, beside the switch, was a slug. It was crawling up the wall. He recoiled in disgust. He put the mug and the glass down and reached for a piece of kitchen tissue. He approached the slimy mollusc timidly. It was large and the colour of shit, with glistening rivulets along its length. He took it in the tissue and squelched it in his fingers. He could feel its body pop open beneath his thumb. He placed the tissue in the bin and washed his hands. He switched off the light and slowly, in darkness, made his way back up to the bedroom.

In the kitchen, his hot mug of tea steamed next to the ice cold glass of Vimto.

Jogging

Peter Bromley

My house is a car park now. I still think of it as my house, even though Sue moved in just before we were married. Terraced houses packed tight as allotment cabbages. Snug back-to-backs. Cooky, the widow who lived opposite us would always sense when we had the drinks out.

'Beer, Cooky?'

'Don't mind if I do.'

'Have a seat.'

'I won't stop…'

…and she would still be there when we served dinner, by which time she had usually had three or four drinks. She would leave in a waving of arms and high drama. She refused to vacate her house when the streets were purchased as part of a strategic site development plan - a by-pass which never happened. But eventually even her house was boarded-up and then demolished. She gave us a small holly tree, though, which we keep in a pot in our tiny back garden.

We are taking the children to the new sports centre. From the upper deck of the bus, Sue and I point out the former street patterns and peoples' houses to our children. I try to show them where our house was and where Cooky's was too. They cannot understand. They just want to get to the centre and swim in the waves generated by the wave machine.

As I look out from the bus, I notice the small change in the colour of the concrete which marks the point at which our front room became the street. Audis, BMWs, Fords; they all park there oblivious to the significance of the change in surface material. The ticket machine stands in our back kitchen.

We got married, Sue and I, because it just seemed right. Before that we lived together. For a while we lived in the house that is now just a series of blots and scars on the car park surface. Cooky knew that we weren't married. All she said was 'Glad to see you made it legal' and winked when we arrived home from work one evening, a week after we got married.

The time I first met Sue, Neil Mitchell stole half a bottle of vodka from his dad's drinks cabinet after school.

'He'll miss it, Neil.' I said.

'He won't.'

'It's not legal.'

'He won't miss it, he's too stupid. Besides, what if he does?'

He had it in the inside pocket of his new leather jacket, snug as a gun. It was a time when we thought that there were more girls in the world than we could decently imagine. All those girls and half a bottle of vodka too so we went to the Hoppings Fair. We swaggered through the muddy fields and crowds.

During the day we watched police dogs and marching bands. We laughed at the womens' gymnastic display. We danced and messed around at the edge of the roped-off arena. We pushed each other and pointed at the women. Dave Briggs fell on his arse in the mud. Then there were the Morris Men…we shouted at them until an old man in a blue blazer and a badge that said 'Steward' told us to stop.

'Come on,' said Neil.

'Where?'

'To the rides.'

'This is crap!'

'Lets get some hot dogs.'

'I need a piss.'

We went for hot dogs. I had my first drink of vodka. It choked me, so from then on I only pretended to drink it, simply holding it to my lips and tilting the bottle back. I let out a sigh and wiped my mouth with my sleeve each time I faked a drink.

'Watch this,' said Dave.

He paid his money and was handed three darts which he fired off with wild windmill arms. Wham. Wham.Wham. Not one of them hit the tightly-packed playing cards he was aiming at.

'Tosser,' said Neil.

'Yeah, tosser,' I added.

Dave pushed me, 'You do better. Come on.'

Across the grubby field the shanty town of the fair was beginning to light up. By now, most of the families were leaving. The people left were mostly couples or groups like us. The dodgems were surrounded by people that were all about our age. The fairground attendants were chatting up groups of girls. One of the attendants, a boy younger than me, had tattoos around his neck and tattoos up both arms. The girls he was talking to were laughing nervously. One of them put her hand up to her mouth to giggle. Eventually the girls moved off, only briefly looking back over their shoulders as they laughed and jostled with each other. The boy shouted something like, 'You don't know what you're missing' and began to talk to some other girls.

'Look. There's Mandy,' said Neil.

'Randy Mandy.'

He pointed with his half-empty bottle of vodka to a group of girls who were getting into some of the dodgems.

'I had her once.' He hadn't. I knew that. We all knew that. But none of us said anything. 'She's with her mates. Come on.'

We pushed our way into two dodgem cars and began driving after the girls. As we chased them Neil drank from his bottle and tried to pass it to me but was seen by one of the attendants and he put it back in his jacket pocket.

After we got off, Dave Briggs simply shouted, 'Hey Mandy,' and it was that easy. We were talking to them. Mandy took a drink; a real drink. Her mate, Sue Trenarry, took a drink too. She passed the bottle to me.

'You're Sue, aren't you?' I said.

'Smooth,' said Dave, butting in to take the vodka.

'Where are you going?'

'Nowhere.'

'Come on with that vodka.'

'Let's go to the rifle range.'

'Let's get Dave to teach us to play darts.'

'Piss off!'

'Piss off yourself.'

We all walked, not sure of where we were heading. I tried to walk next to Sue. Neil passed me the almost empty bottle of vodka and I took a drink. I almost choked. I passed it to Sue.

'No thanks. I can't stand it,' she said.

'But you had a drink before.'

'No I didn't. I faked it.'

'I've seen you at the bus station.'

'I've seen you too. With your mate Neil.'

'I bet you fancy him.'

'Not really. He's a big head.'

We walked behind the others and then let them move further away.

'Want a hot dog?' I asked.

'Yeah. Why not?'

'Hey Neil. We're going for a hot dog,' I shouted.

The others turned around and jeered but kept walking.

As Sue and I walked through the mud, her shoes kept slipping off. Eventually she put her arm through mine. 'I keep slipping,' she explained, briefly looking at me then returning her gaze to the ground ahead.

Later, on a bench under the dripping trees, we kissed. It happened just like that. Kissing Sue Trenarry. My God! I was kissing Sue Trenarry.

On the bus home I sat downstairs with Sue.

'What are you doing when you leave school?'

'Don't know,' I said.

'No idea?'

'I might do a trade.' After a pause, I added, 'Engineering or something. What about you?'

'I want to go and stay with my sister,' she said. 'She's got a flat and a job in London. She says I can go there for a while. I don't know really. I think I might like to go to college.'

And, as I held her hand, my mind swooped from the empty damp bus through the deserted street down motorways I had never seen and settled on my own vision of London. There it rested for the remainder of our journey.

Walking from Sue's bus stop we wove through back alleys and streets on her council estate. We passed a row of shuttered shops, with cars outside, parked half on the pavement. Behind the houses lay a deep silence. At her door I kissed her.

'I'd invite you in but my dad's probably still up,' she said.

'It's alright.'

'How'll you get home?'

'I'll walk.'

And we kissed again. Bloody hell! Kissing Sue Trenarry. I tried to move my hands onto her bum, but she moved them back around her waist.

'You've had too much vodka.'

'Can I ring you?' I asked.

'If you want.'

She took out her key and opened the door. She kissed me then put her finger to her lips to tell me to be quiet. She turned and went into the house.

I walked to the end of the street. At first I walked just on the pavement. Then I ran with one foot on the pavement and one foot in the gutter. I ran past the barking dogs, passed the row of shops, the parked cars and down the hill, happier than I had ever been.

After our house became a car park, Sue and I moved to our new house. It's in a new development. Lots of low-rise units. It doesn't have any real shops near it. There's a video shop, a car accessory shop, a gym, and a tanning centre. There used to be a butcher, though. If I'd been asked to draw a butcher when I was six or seven I would have drawn Clive, who used to run the shop. Fat, red-faced and sort of funny. He worked hard at his humour, did Clive. For days he used a one-liner, getting the emphasis right; honing up the timing. Then it got used until it was blunt and useless and finally disposed of. He had a large plastic model of a butcher outside his shop, about half as big again as Clive. Dressed in a blue and white striped apron and a boater, the model was chained to Clive's drainpipe. Some of the local kids wrote on the model in black felt tip pen 'Fat Bastard Clive.'

All through the scare about mad-cow disease, Clive ate British beef. 'Well I would, wouldn't I?' he said. He even had some small pieces on a plate on his counter. Periodically he would dip into it and chew away at a lump of roast beef.

'Come on you lot. Safe as houses,' he would say.

'My house was demolished,' I said. 'Turned into a car park.'

He kept threatening to leave. 'There's life in the old dog yet,' he would say, grinning at the old women in the queue. Then he was gone. The shop unit was up for sale and within a week he had transferred his business to an older shop in a block of terraces across town. Victoria Street; near the motorway link road. He left his fat friend chained to the drainpipe. Within a day it had been smashed open and had been filled up with litter. A hairdresser moved into the unit and it is now called 'Sizzers 'n' Combs'. He said, 'Victoria Street has lost more character than this new development will ever have.'

Sue, me and the children arrive at the sports centre on the bus. The children rush off to get changed. As they bob up and down in the false waves, I stand on the balcony in the main hall watching Sue work out in the step aerobics class. The women all stare ahead to the large mirror on the wall and eventually back to themselves in its reflection. The woman at the front of the class has a microphone on a head-set and a small radio transmitter attached to the back of her lycra shorts. Seeing her reminds me how unfit I have become. After we have finished at the centre and on our way back to the bus station, I buy a pair of cheap running shoes; I need to do something. At home I put on the shoes and squeeze into an old tracksuit of Sue's. And I run.

Sometimes I walk but mostly I run. I run down our street. Past the row of shops, past posters for the Hoppings Fair, past advertisements for cheap flights to Barcelona, Dublin, and London. Then I run to the car park and run around my old house. Past the television into the kitchen and into the back yard. Back inside the house again and up the stairs. Into the bedroom where

Sue and I made love illegally and then, according to Cooky, legally. Then into the bathroom where we had stared into the pregnancy testing kit that was showing positive. 'That's our baby,' I had said and Sue had cried.

And then I run out of the house and off towards the motorway. For a while, I run with one foot on the road and one on the kerb. Then I run along the pavement, over the low bridge by the canal passed where Dave Briggs used to live. And then on, in search of Victoria Street, Fat Bastard Clive and much more besides.

Why I have to wear a pair of Wranglers everyday for as long as I live on this street

James Walker

A battered Mini plods down our street doing around 25mph. The speed is dictated more by the inadequacy of its engine than conformity to speed limits. A dog runs out under the car; straight into the side of the wheel. You can hear the thump as it clogs up the air like a painful gulp. Some kids stop playing football and I can hear them shout, 'the fucking dog's been hit.' They stare ahead, too far away for altruism to grab at their conscience, and continue to play football. I hear one say that it's not his dog; another declares his mum won't let him have one. Soon both are laughing giving the impression that this is a natural occurrence on our street.

The Mini pauses momentarily then proceeds on its journey. The gears grind, symbolising the driver's unease. I stop and stare at the dog as it's only a few yards away and then stare at the car driving off into the distance; its smoke polluting the air, indicating either a rusting exhaust or perhaps an oil change is required. It is irrelevant; such duties will only be performed on MOT day when legally required. For now the car performs its perfunctory obligation in getting the driver back home.

My first thought is do I leave the dog as the Mini has? My second is I wish I was playing football with the kids. My third is I wish I wasn't a vegetarian because now I feel morally implicated. I don't even like animals, I just don't eat them. Why I should feel guilty about eating something I care nothing for I will never know, but this is neither here nor there as I am here and the dog is laying there. There is nobody around I can turn to for advice and so I light up a cigarette and watch the smoke drift up towards the sky. As usual I am caught in a situation which never popped up on the syllabus at school.

As I extinguish my cigarette I hope the dog is not stuck to the floor. I don't want to have to peel it off the road and listen to that Velcro noise it will make. I feel a little bad that this is my initial reaction, which in comparison with the dog's life, or lack of it, is hardly a concern. Then I imagine how I would have reacted if it had been a child. I imagine I would have continued smoking and the Mini would have driven off a little faster, and the kids may have used the body as a goalpost. The last thing in the world an injured dog needs is someone locked away in his imagination, then again the last thing the dog really needed was to be hit by a Mini.

A child is at an adjacent window staring out. He has not seen the incident but has heard a noise which has aroused intrigue. His mother comes to the window, knocking the child's head with her breast as she leans forward, before closing the curtain and resuming her position in front of the television.

I walk over to the dog because it is getting dark. If another car comes along and runs over it again I am never going to be able to peel it off the tarmac. As I close in I consider obtaining some chalk and drawing around its body. Fortunately I have no chalk at hand which forces me to take more productive action.

I considered taking it into the house with me. Putting it on the table where the TV should be, and telling mother I have brought her an inexpensive pet; one that does not need feeding or walking, a polite pet that will never bite the postman or shit on the carpet. It is an inoffensive pet that will lie next to her on the sofa and never tire of being stroked, the perfect pet for an imperfect and lazy generation. Then again perhaps I should just dump it inside the wheelie bin. I think they collect on a Thursday.

Instead I have another cigarette.

Once I ran over a snake. It was black and at first I thought it was a stick or the inner valve of a bicycle tyre. In hindsight, as far as road-kills go, it is up there with the best. You are hard fetched to find one in a field let alone slivering across the slow lane of the A52. I reversed to confirm my suspicions and although I knew it was dead I just wanted to look at it. As I wound my window down a crow made a noise and then perched upon a tree. As it squawked, I felt as if it was telling me not to worry. That it would sort out the mess. I wish that crow was here now.

Perhaps because I had run out of cigarettes I was forced into action. I edged forwards and inspected the animal, not too sure if I should stroke it or give it mouth-to-mouth resuscitation. Suddenly the dog moves and it lets out the most delayed and pained scream I have ever heard. It is like it has sucked in the entire pain of the universe and it can bear the weight no more.

Arrrrrrraagggggggggghhhhhhhhhwwooooooooofehhhhhhh.

Now I'm not exaggerating, that's exactly what it was like. It went fucking nuts. I could feel the total confusion, the pain and the frustration all juxtaposed into one deafening scream, more eloquent than if it'd been able to speak.

The dog proceeded to bound around in a circle whilst continuing its scream. It seemed to be intent on catching its tail as if this was culpable for the pain. The fact that it could not catch it seemed to frustrate it more and before I knew what was happening I became its surrogate tail. Suddenly it ran at me, diving through the air, before biting me in the nuts and bolting over the nearest garden fence. Fortunately I had on a pair of particularly tight Wranglers so its fangs couldn't penetrate beyond undoing a seam on my flies.

Such ingratitude.

It would have been fun explaining that one to a future girlfriend.

255

If it is not bad enough that I live with my mum, nearing thirty, unemployed and divorced without the added allure of having only half a penis due to a crazy dog. It is no wonder the kids continued to play football as the Mini drove on and that there are no crows around. Only an idiot would stop to give help.

I went back to my place and got another packet of cigarettes as I tried to figure out which one of the neighbours' dogs it was. Nowadays I don't even know which one of the kids belongs to which neighbour let alone which pets. You don't see anybody about anymore. Only kids playing football and the occasional parent struggling with ripped Co-Op bags down the road.

I knock on a few doors. Nobody knows who owns the dog but everybody wants to know why I want to know. I try to explain the howling noise it made and how it tried to bite my nuts but they just look at me like I am a pervert so I apologise for bothering them. As I make my way down the street they hang on to their front doors tracing my footsteps. They look like dominoes, all waiting to fall back inside their doors once a reason has been ascertained. I wonder if they would be so interested if *Eastenders* was on.

Finally a woman answers a door and admits to owning a black dog. She has a baby in her hand and immediately hands the baby to the husband. He sniffs at its nappy as if he has been set up.

'Don't worry. But I have some bad news.'

I watch the woman's face turn from a pale brown to a red, before settling on white.

'Your dog ran out in the road...'

Before I can finish she lunges at me and I feel her nails claw into my neck. One becomes lodged in my ear and I realise they are false and probably quite expensive. Then she kicks me in the nuts and I see what they mean about owners resembling their pets. She tells me I am a wanker and I should drive more carefully and then punches me so I fall back on to the floor. Within seconds she is sat on my chest and as she screams, drops of spittle fall from her mouth and land inside mine which for some strange reason, I find quite erotic. Her husband ignores the behaviour as if it is commonplace and seems only to be concerned as to why he is still holding the baby. He sniffs at the nappy again and when he can smell nothing becomes suspicious.

His wife punches me in the nuts again as if evolutionary knowledge states that this is the only way to defeat a man. Once more I am grateful for my skin-tight Wranglers that serve as armour and thankful I am not a slave to fashion, as baggies would have served as poor protection.

'Dog killer…that was our child's pet…poor Benji.'

There is no point explaining to her that I did not run over the dog. Sometimes it is like this in life, but through habit rather than choice, I try to explain.

'Your dog is alive.'

'You sick bastard. You liar. What kind of thing do you get off on?'

She is now stood above me and kicks me in the nuts. This time I feel something and a strange melting in my stomach takes place like when you leave butter near a window and it turns to a salty liquid. The seam has obviously taken its last blow and is now caving in. I will have to take them back and complain.

'The dog hit the side of the wheel. It ran in a circle howling and then leaped over that fence. It was a massive jump, like a horse in the Grand National.'

She continues kicking, proving that women have the potential to be as good as men at football.

'I figured the dog must be from around here as it ran off near your house. I just figured I should tell someone, as it may be curled up somewhere in pain. It's not like it can go to a doctor or tell someone what's happened.'

She runs off, shouting 'Benji, my darling' and then back towards me. 'You bastard.' Sometimes due to her distress she shouts 'You bastard' in the direction of Benji, whilst calling me 'My darling', something I chose not to point out.

The father walks over to me. 'I hated that fucking dog. I bet it's still alive as well. It's always pissing on the floor. You don't want to be slipping in piss after a day at work. Sometimes I think she cares more for the dog than me.'

The baby changes colour and a smell emanates from its nappy. The man shakes his head. 'Kids and fucking dogs. It's all shit and piss.' He calls after his wife and when she returns he presents her with the baby, and its shit, and she starts to cry. But not before reminding me once more that I have completely destroyed her child's happiness by killing the family pet. I do not bother to point out that the dog is still alive or that the child is so young it will have forgotten by bedtime. Instead I make my way home.

When Mother came home she asked me if I had had a good day, and like all children I told her exactly what she needed to hear; yes I had and that life was just dandy. She then had a go at me for ruining my jeans and asked me how I was going to replace them when I had no job or money. Was I expecting her to pay for a new pair when she hardly had any money as it was? I told her I was going to sew them up but she demanded them off me. If anyone was going to do any sewing it was going to be her. What did I know about sewing? And so I disrobed and presented her the damaged Wranglers, thinking to myself that I never envisaged standing in front of my mother at twenty-eight in my pants having her still look after me.

After that day every time I saw that bloody dog it would run at me and try to bite me. Over time it became less fixated on my nuts and seemed to settle for any bodily part it could sink its teeth in to. I suppose we all settle for second best in the end and that this is better than nothing. The Wranglers served as ample protection and I soon found myself buying a jacket to match so my arms and chest had similar protection. Meeting a girl I accepted would now be impossible, unless they were into double denim.

Strangest of all was after biting me everyday the dog would still run in a circle and then leap over an adjacent fence. It was as if it had been given a new role in life, a new perspective. I don't know if it thought it was a horse or if it thought it could fly now, but it certainly seemed happier. Maybe its near death experience gave it a new lease of life, no longer constrained by the limitations of its species. But to be perfectly honest, it was me who was experiencing the possibility of death each time I left the house as its owner continued to attack me as well.

Over time I have come to accept that it will be hard to persuade future girlfriends that I am a good person whilst being constantly attacked by my neighbour and her pet. Besides, it's never really ever that bad. As a result of running away from Benji and his owner I have lost a little weight and am reasonably fit. Perhaps when I have reached my peak fitness I will keep on running until I find a neighbourhood of sensible adults and sensible pets and drivers that are more careful on roads.

Biographies

Malcolm Aslett was born in South Shields and grew up in the North East though he has spent much of his adult life abroad. He is married and presently lives in Buckinghamshire.

Peter Bromley lives in Northumberland. As well as having work published in *Route 14*, he has had short fiction published in Chapman, the Echo Room and has won a number of awards, including the 2004 Biscuit Publication competition and a New Writing North Northern Promise award. He is currently putting together a collection of short stories.

Mark Costello was born in Batley, 1969. After being a biscuit packer, aluminium fabricator and care assistant, he decided to get educated. A few years later having gained a degree in Sociology and training as a Careers Adviser then Teacher, he met a princess called Cathryn had a son called Bram moved to Cumbria and had a daughter called Dory. All four now live in the middle of a sheep field up the side of a fell. This is Mark's first attempt at short story writing. He may write another.

Steve Dearden was writer-in-residence at Bluewater Shopping Centre as part of www.architexts.org and is currently one of three Yorkshire based writers working with three from Ostrobothnia, Finland on *Interland*, a watery tour and publication. He runs the National Association for Literature Development and the Writing Squad for writers aged 16-20. Visit www.stevedearden.com

Penny Feeny is an award-winning short story writer whose work has appeared widely in print, on radio and online. Her publication credits include *Atlantic Monthly*, *Mslexia*, *Staple* and *The Reader* as well as Arc's *Northern Stories* anthology and Tindal Street's *Her Majesty*.

She has lived and worked in various cities: Cambridge, Bristol, London and Rome, but has been settled for many years now in Liverpool with her family.

Jane Graham is bitten by a certain wanderlust and, at the point of publication, resides in Denmark. Previous works include *Floozy* (published in 1997 by Slab-O-Concrete), a series of sometimes funny, often nerve-racking adventures around the more grubby haunts of the north of England, *Kitchen Sink* which appeared in the anthology *Brit Pulp!* in 1999, and the self-published zine *Shag Stamp* produced throughout the nineties and still remembered among zinesters. She is also a regular contributor to the underground periodical *Headpress. Expectanz* was written shortly after giving birth to her first child.

Lee James Harrison was born and bound to the Nation-State of Kingston-upon-Hull. From a young age, he tried to write about monsters and baddies, rather than deal with his life. 'I nearly might have had a story made into a film' he screams. More stories and an attempt at a novel are forthcoming. He has no spare time, but is often seen staggering along the fish-paved streets of Hull wearing a paisley tuxedo, speaking in a badly dubbed voice and spraying Lynx at gullible tourists.

Mandy MacFarlane is from Dundee and has lived in Leeds for the last eleven years. She is currently putting together a collection of short stories for publication.

Char March is an award-winning poet and playwright. Credits include: three collections of poetry, five BBC Radio 4 plays and seven stage plays. She has also been published widely in literary magazines and anthologies here and in the States. Char is currently working on her fourth poetry collection and her first novel. She grew up in Scotland and now divides her time between the Highlands and Yorkshire.

James Nash grew up in West London. He came to Leeds University in 1971 to do an MA in English and Anglo-Irish literature. Having taught for many years in inner-city schools, he now works as a journalist and writer, editing a poetry column in *The Leeds Guide*. His third collection of poems *Coma Songs* was published in 2003 to great acclaim. He is writer-in-residence for Leeds University, Faculty of Education, and for High Schools in Calderdale. He also teaches creative writing at HM Prison Wakefield, and hosts many literary events across the country.

Tom Palmer was born in Leeds. He is the author of *If You're Proud to be a Leeds Fan, The Bradford Wool Exchange* and several short stories. He has written for various newspapers, including the *Observer*. He is the editor of *FourFathers* to be published by Route-online. He is currently working on his novel, *News Junky*, for which he received the K Blundell Award. Tom is a freelance reader development worker and lives in Todmorden with his wife and daughter.

Andrew Parker lives in Liverpool and has had a handful of short stories published.

Adrian Reynolds started his life in Birmingham, and gradually made his way to Nottingham. He is primarily a scriptwriter, with numerous stage credits, has written episodes of *Doctors* for the BBC, and devised feature film treatments for production companies. Adrian also runs workshops on scriptwriting and other forms of creativity and communication. His email address is adrian.reynolds@ntlworld.com

Dee Rimbaud is an artist and writer, living in Glasgow, Scotland, but will soon be packing his bags and heading off to sunnier climes. He is author of two full-length collections of poetry and one novel: *The Bad Seed* (Stride, 1998), *Dropping Ecstasy With The Angels* (Bluechrome, 2004), and *Stealing Heaven From The Lips Of God* (Bluechrome, 2004). He is editor of *The AA Independent Press Guide* and *The Book Of Hopes And Dreams*. Further information on all of these can be found at www.thunderburst.co.uk

Tajinder Singh Hayer is a 23 year-old Bradfordian. He has had poems and short stories published in magazines, several short plays put on at the West Yorkshire Playhouse, and has had a short radio drama produced by the BBC. Most recently he has been a writer-in-residence at the West Yorkshire Playhouse. He has completed an MA in Creative Writing at the University of Leeds and also teaches Creative Writing at the University of Bradford.

Michael Stewart is an award winning writer, born and dragged up in Salford, who moved to Yorkshire in 1995 and is now based in Bradford. He has written several full length stage plays, as well as securing work in radio and television; most recently writing for *Emmerdale*. He was the winner of the BBC Alfred Bradley Award in 2003 and is currently finishing a commission for Pilot Theatre Company. His stage plays have been performed across the country. His new play *Xrossing the Line*, will premiere next year at the Courtyard Theatre in London.

James Walker has written freelance and fiction for numerous publications. In 2003 he won the Jo Cowell Award. His first novel *This is All I Know* is due for publication with Pomona in spring 2005. For information on his second novel *The Problem with William. G. Stewart and Hoovers* and other work please visit www.jameskwalker.com When James is not writing he likes to play football with the kids on his street, but refuses to go in goal.

The Route Series

*Route publishes a regular series of titles
for which it offers an annual subscription.*

Naked City (Route 15) is a title in the Route Series.
For details of the current subscription scheme
and our complete book list please visit:

www.route-online.com

Jack and Sal

Anthony Cropper

ISBN 1-901927 21 0 £8.95

Jack and Sal, two people drifting in and out of love. Jack searches for clues, for a pattern, for an explanation to life's events. Perhaps the answer is in evolution, in dopamine, in chaos theory, or maybe it can be found in the minutiae of domesticity where the majority of life's dramas unfold. Here, Anthony Cropper has produced a delicately detailed account of a troubled relationship, with a series of micro-stories and incidents that recount the intimate lies, loves and lives of Jack and Sal and their close friend Paula.

Next Stop Hope - Route 14

ISBN 1-901927 19 9 £6.95

A title in the route series, presented in three distinct collections: *Criminally Minded, Something Has Gone Wrong in the World* and *Next Stop Hope*. Featuring new short fiction and poetry from thirty-three writers.

Warehouse

MS Green, Alan Green, Clayton Devanny, Simon Nodder, Jono Bell - Ed Ian Daley

ISBN 1-901927 10 5 £6.95

Warehouse is a unique type of social realism, written by young warehouse operatives from the bottom end of the labour market in the middle of the post-industrial heartland, it steps to the beat of modern day working-class life. A soundtrack to the stories is included on a complimentary CD, warehouse blues supplied by *The Chapter* and urban funk grooves from *Budists*

One Northern Soul

J R Endeacott

ISBN 1-901927 17 2 £5.95

If that goal in Paris had been allowed then everything that followed could have been different. For young Stephen Bottomley something died that night. *One Northern Soul* follows the fortunes of this Leeds United fan as he comes of age in the dark days of the early eighties.

The Unexpected Pond

Ed - Chris Firth

ISBN 1-901927 05 9 £5

Twenty stories to unsettle the complacent mind. This is a collection that is both challenging and healing. The Unexpected Pond is a book to unlock the imagination with a collection of stories focused on the bizarre, outlandish and macabre. These stories with their unexpected twists, turns and unusual premise, take the reader to the extremities of the mind and back again, through darkness into light.

Tubthumping

Ed - Adrian Wilson

ISBN 1-901927 17 2 £6.95

Pioneering short story collection that was the initial force behind the Route imprint. Human preoccupations - love and hate, anger and betrayal, lust and longing - are played out against a panoramic backdrop that would have been inconceivable before now. With an introduction by Alice Nutter.